"How can you r
continued, ey
A pioneer, braving un
worlds and new—"

"If you split an infinitive, I'm leaving," Nashira told him. "You think this job is glamorous? Some big adventure you can tag along on? Let me tell you something. Space isn't empty. Space is beyond empty. At least 'empty' implies there's something there that can be filled. Space is nothing, with trace impurities.

"Now, imagine jumping randomly into nothing for a living. Imagine the odds of happening to materialize in range of one of those trace impurities, one that's interesting enough that people might want to come to it. Can you imagine that?" He thought it over, and she interrupted before he could speak. "I'll give you the answer: You can't. Whatever you're imagining, it's not even close.

"Now, imagine knowing that if you do eventually find a Hubpoint that's close to a star or planet, there's no way to know you won't emerge directly inside it and get an instant, no-fuss burial or cremation thrown in free with your death. Not that I'm complaining; that undercurrent of mortal terror before every dive helped relieve the monotony for the first year or so."

"And now?"

"Now it offers a ray of hope."

Copyright © 2017 by Christopher L. Bennett
ISBN 978-1-946025-49-4
All rights reserved. No part of this book may be used or reproduced in any manner whatsoever without written permission except in the case of brief quotations embodied in critical
articles and reviews
For information address Crossroad Press at 141 Brayden Dr., Hertford, NC 27944
A Mystique Press Production - Mystique Press is an imprint of Crossroad Press.
www.crossroadpress.com

First edition

HUB SPACE
TALES FROM THE GREATER GALAXY

BY CHRISTOPHER L. BENNETT

CONTENTS

THE HUB OF THE MATTER	1
HOME IS WHERE THE HUB IS	35
MAKE HUB, NOT WAR	71
AFTERWORD: MAKE YOURSELF AT HUB	107

ACKNOWLEDGMENTS

"The Hub of the Matter" in *Analog Science Fiction and Fact*, Vol. CXXX No. 3 (March 2010), pp. 76-88.
"Home is Where the Hub Is" in *Analog Science Fiction and Fact*, Vol. CXXX No. 12 (December 2010), pp. 70-85.
"Make Hub, Not War" in *Analog Science Fiction and Fact*, Vol. CXXXIII No. 11 (November 2013), pp. 24-38.

THE HUB OF THE MATTER

1

It is a universal law that the faster a mode of transportation is, the more extreme its associated delays become. The Hub offered instantaneous travel to anywhere in the galaxy, so its gridlock achieved truly cosmic proportions.

The wait might not have been so bad for David LaMacchia if he hadn't been seated in the midst of a family-pod of Hijjeg tourists returning home from Earth. He'd expected everything in space to be grander than it was back home, but he hadn't expected that to include his personal curse that the fattest individual on the bus—or in this case, the members of the largest, smelliest species—always sat next to him. *My first lesson in galactic travel: from now on, take the aisle seat.*

If not for the Hijjeg group, the passenger transport would have been relatively empty. The only other passengers were a half-dozen fellow humans en route to a medical conference to plead for aid, a sub-clan of Poviqq migrant workers who'd found better employment in another system, and a group of L'myekist missionaries returning home with a large haul of tithes from their human converts. (L'myekism required abandoning all worldly possessions—leading David to wonder how the missionaries had reserved the first-class compartment, and why they seemed so enormously amused with themselves.) The Hijjeg were the only tourists in the group, having come to Earth to enjoy its high levels of atmospheric sulfur dioxide while they still had the chance.

Once the transport finally got clearance to enter the Sol System Hubpoint, the surrounding bulk of Hijjeg flesh and the watering of David's eyes made him miss the split-second transition to the Hub itself. Nonetheless, a thrill went through him, for he knew that he was *here*—just south of the far end of the galactic bar, forty thousand light-years from home. A place no human had ever imagined was reachable until a mere seven years before his birth, when the first Network scout ships had come through the Hubpoint and brought the whole galaxy to humanity.

But he was still surrounded by Hijjeg and losing the feeling in his crushed extremities. The wait was even greater at this end, for as the only means of faster-than-light travel known to exist—the single point that every interstellar ship had to pass through to get anywhere—the Hub was, admittedly, something of a bottleneck. It took longer for the shuttle to get out of the surrounding Shell and into open space than it did to cross the hundreds of kilometers to the vast ring habitat that housed its destination.

Finally the transport docked at Hubstation 3742, serving Earth and worlds of comparable biochemistry and socioeconomic status. David found himself bustled off the shuttle by the press of Hijjeg bodies before he'd fully managed to restore circulation to his limbs. The L'myekist monks were just ahead of him, cackling drunkenly to one another. *This is it*, he thought as his luggage caught up with him after a frantic search, rubbing against his leg and offering up its handle. *Here is the place where I begin my quest.*

It looked uncannily like a bus station. Smelled like one too, but with aromatic overtones unknown on Earth. David's shoulders slumped. "This is the Hub?"

"What is to expect?" rumbled the largest of his Hijjeg seatmates as it trundled past, family-pod in tow. "Low-rung world like yours getting *good* facilities? You want it, you earn it."

His doubts evaporating, he gave the opinionated hillock a defiant smile. "My friend, that's exactly what I'm here to do."

The Hijjeg rumbled. "Good luck. My world try for six generations. Still stuck in this dump."

"Thanks!" David replied. "Good luck to you too."

As he navigated the crowd, David was thrilled to see so many exotic kinds of life in more types of mask, suit, exoskeleton, and other life-support mechanisms than he could identify. This particular Hubstation catered mainly to oxygen-breathing bipeds, but business and tourism transcended most environmental categories. The wonder of the sights more than made up for the smells.

Finally he found the lobby area for the Hubstation's hotel—about thirty meters past the end of the line for the registration desk. He napped on the back of his trunk until it finally reached the desk, and it gave a whirr of relief when he climbed off and stretched his limbs. "Boy, this place is busy! I hope you still have some empty rooms. I'm exhausted."

The desk clerk, a cadaverous, blue-skinned Jiodeyn, peered at him with four small black eyes. "Empty rooms, sir? No, sir, we have none currently."

"Oh." David slumped. "Then where am I going to sleep?"

"We have a number of rooms available, sir."

Huh? "But you just said there were no rooms."

"No empty rooms, that's correct, sir."

"Wait... you mean I'd have to share a room?"

"No, sir. You would have your own space."

"Space. I'd just have part of the room?"

"One segment, sir, but you would have the full space."

He blinked. "Do we take turns?"

"No, sir, you may stay as long as you wish." The clerk looked him over. "Provided you can pay."

"But other people will be in the room."

The Jiodeyn spoke as if he were doing David a favor by being so patient. "Each suite accommodates seven, sir."

"O... kay." David had lived with roommates before, during his college career—all five months of it—and he doubted any of them would be as interesting as the aliens he could meet here. "So there are seven beds per room?"

"No, sir, just the one."

"For *seven people?*" he cried.

"We don't pry into how our customers use their beds, sir," the clerk replied primly.

"Isn't that kind of... well... cramped?"

"Our beds are quite roomy, sir."

"They'd have to be," David muttered. Feeling a bit dizzy, he tried a different tack. "Look, what about life support? You wouldn't put an ammonia-breather or a silicone life form in the same suite with me, right?"

The clerk glared. "Sir, this establishment does not discriminate."

"But that would kill me!"

"Not necessarily, sir, since you have not chosen a room yet."

David took a breath and spoke very carefully. "Okay. Look. Do you have any rooms occupied only by species whose life-support needs wouldn't kill me?"

The Jiodeyn checked his computer with two of his four arms. "Suite forty-seven currently holds five oxygen-breathers and one chlorine-breather. That is the best we can do at this time, sir."

"Does the chlorine-breather wear a mask or something?"

"Not in his room, sir."

David gasped. "Then how am I supposed to not die?!"

"That will be no problem, sir, so long as you stay in your own room."

"But you said he's in the room too!"

"Yes, sir. Would you like me to page him?"

"I don't know," David said, shaking his head. "What page are we even on?"

A new voice spoke. "That room will be fine for my friend here, Yolien. Put it on my account."

David turned to see a tall, elegant, relatively humanoid biped with tawny skin, handsome leonine features, and a mane of golden feathers down his back. No surprise, he thought, that a Sosyryn would come to his rescue.

The clerk took it in stride. "Very good, Mr. Rynyan. Here is your key, sir." He handed David a small crystal rod.

At the Sosyryn's prompting, David took the key, but he was still confused. "But what about—"

"You're new to the Hub, aren't you?" Rynyan asked as he led David aside. At the human's nod, he continued. "The rooms are tesseracts, you see. They use a quirk of the spacetime around the Hub to extend into four dimensions. Eight cubic 'faces,' making for seven rooms and one entry interface. The only way the Hub complex can handle the volume of traffic, you see."

David was beginning to catch on. "So the key…"

"Rotates the interface to the particular room it's associated with. You use that key and you'll have no worries about opening the wrong room, inhaling chlorine, and dying in agony as your mucus turns into hydrochloric acid." He paused. "Well, so long as the interface doesn't malfunction. The maintenance crews don't get out here as often as they could," he went on with no change to his breezy, reassuring tone. David looked warily at the key.

"Ah! I've been rude. I am Rynyan Zynara ad Surynyyyyyy'a. Welcome, traveler, to the Hub."

David shook his hand. "Hi. David LaMacchia."

"Human, right?" Rynyan asked. "From Earth?"

"And proud of it."

"Good for you! I suppose someone has to be. I've taken an interest in your planet, you know. That's why I'm slumming here—I'd been hoping to meet someone interesting from Earth. Are you interesting?"

"That's what I'm here to find out."

"Good answer! You humans have such clever ways of saying 'no.' Well, Earth is a lovely world anyway," he went on before David could answer. "Shame about the climatic catastrophes, though. They must be terribly inconvenient."

"Uhh… thanks. Really, we'd be much worse off if it weren't for all your people's help."

Rynyan spread his arms magnanimously. "It's our purpose in this universe. I mean, we have no problems of our own, so we need to have them imported." He gave a passing imitation of a human laugh. "I joke. Seriously, your world was fortunate to be discovered when it was. Rysos was in similarly dire straits millennia ago. Then contact with the Hub Network and its advances and wealth let us make our world the paradise it is today. It is our privilege to share our… well, our privilege with others who are less… privileged." He tapped his neck, where he presumably kept the implant that translated his speech impulses into the language of his choice before they reached his mouth. "That can't be quite right."

"I really admire your people," David said as Rynyan led him toward his room, his trunk scuttling wearily behind. "You're so egalitarian. You have so much, but it isn't hoarded by a greedy few. You make sure everyone benefits from it."

"The gratitude of others is our wealth," the Sosyryn replied. "Now, let me do something *really* generous for you. My cousin just endowed an orphanage, and I'll never live it down if I let that uncultured boor out-donate me."

"Oh, no, I couldn't. The room is fine."

"Come now, there must be something. What is it you hope to gain here at the Hub?"

David's eyes lit up. "It's been my mission in life to get here. I didn't have much growing up, but I always believed that I—that humans—were capable of better. There's a whole galaxy out there, just on the other side of the Hub, and that's where humanity's future lies. Where my future lies. It cost me all my savings just to get a ticket off-world. And now I'm here."

"What a charming story. And now that you're here, what will you do next? Or do you plan to kill yourself now that your life's goal is achieved?" he asked with sincere curiosity. "That would be an unconventional thing to help you with, a bit tricky to work into the plus column, but I suppose I could work something out."

But David smiled. "Oh, I've only just begun to chase my life's goal. You see… I'm going to figure out how the Hub works."

"Oh, oh, I can tell you that!" Rynyan said excitedly. "It's at the center of mass of the dark matter halo that encompasses our galaxy and its satellites, and it connects to every point within that halo, so long as you know the right entry vector. All you have to do is dive in at the right speed and angle and—"

"No, no, I know that part!" David said, chuckling. "I mean I'm going to figure out the part nobody else has figured out yet."

Rynyan stared. "You mean the relationship between the Hub vectors and the exit points?"

"Right. I'm going to find the pattern. I'm going to make it

possible to go anywhere in the Galaxy by choice, not just by trial and error."

The Sosyryn gaped at him. "Why, this is delightful! I'd forgotten they haven't yet cured insanity on your world! Do tell me more, this is invigorating!"

David took the comment in stride. "I know it sounds crazy. But somebody's gotta be the one to solve this, and it might as well be a human."

"Oh, this *is* an entertaining delusion! How do you intend to proceed?"

David explained his plan to hire a Hub scout, one of the pilots who took their ships into the Hub on random vectors in the hopes of discovering promising new destinations. It had been such a scout who had stumbled across the Sol System back in 2058; once that vector was logged and recorded, it had allowed steady access to Earth, at least until Sol's drift took it away from the Hubpoint over the next few millennia. But missing the correct vector by a milliarcsecond could send a ship to the other end of the galaxy or a Magellanic Cloud; the relationship wasn't remotely linear, if there even was one. David believed there had to be, and he'd brought instruments that he hoped would prove it. "I just keep collecting data with each jump we make, try to find a pattern. That's why it has to be a Hub scout. They make the most trips."

"You're in luck," Rynyan said. "I just happen to know a very good Hub scout. And she's human, too, so I'm sure she'd be happy to help you out."

"Can you introduce me to her?"

"Absolutely. She positively adores me."

2

"You're an idiot, Rynyan," the Hub scout said.

Her name was Nashira Wing, and she'd spent a lifetime trying to live it down. It was just her rotten luck that she'd turned out to be better at piloting than anything else. "And so is your friend," she went on, "if he thinks he has any chance of cracking the Hub."

Nashira's insult bounced off Rynyan's impenetrable skull as usual, but the Sosyryn stood up for his new pet charity case. "He's not an idiot."

"Thank you," the man named David said.

"He's a lunatic," Rynyan went on, beaming. "I've always wanted one of my own."

Nashira tilted her head to regard him. "Doesn't charity for lunatics involve curing them, not indulging them?"

"Oh, where's the fun in that?"

She turned to the young, sandy-haired human, making an effort to soften her expression. She often welcomed the severity her crisp Asian features and sharp-edged soprano could assume, but this David LaMacchia was a harmless wide-eyed hick who didn't know any better. "Look... David? If there were a way to predict the relationship between entry vectors and exit points, somebody would've done it already. It's what they call an NP-complete problem—there's no way to solve it in a finite amount of time."

"But a solution can be verified in a finite amount of time," David responded, showing that he wasn't completely ignorant about the subject. "If we have a theory to test, we can confirm it."

"And what makes you think you can find a solution nobody else in thousands of planets has thought of? Are you some kind of super-genius?"

"Nope. Just an ordinary human."

"No degrees in astrophysics, quantum physics, anything like that?"

He shook his head. "Don't need 'em." He tapped his face next to his eye. She saw text dancing across his contact lens interface. "A wikigoogler. I've got the sum total of human knowledge at my fingertips. Or... eyetips."

She scoffed. "What?! You think that's gonna give you some special insight?"

"The collective insight of the entire human species," he answered with pride.

"You think that amounts to anything?" She let her face grow severe again, and her voice along with it. "You have no sodding idea what it's really like out here, do you? You don't understand what it means to be in a society with thousands of worlds, with civilizations thousands of times older than ours. I've heard it all—humans wondering why the rest of the galaxy hasn't gone ga-ga over Shakespeare and Mozart and the Grand Canyon and chocolate. It's because the galaxy is just too *big*. Too old. There's too much stuff in it. Everything we have, everything we've ever built or written or thought of, somebody else did it first or has something better. There's nothing new under the stars.

"Why do you think Earth is still so poor after thirty-four years on the Network? Because we have nothing to offer anybody. No reason for them to care about us."

David glanced at Rynyan. "The Sosyryn care."

"Please. Haven't you been listening? You're his new toy. Charity is something Sosyryn do to pass the time. They've wiped out all hardship on their own world, so they're bored stiff looking for something to do."

"You mean," Rynyan corrected with his typical polite condescension, "that we seek to spread the fruits of our prosperity to others."

"So we'll bow down in gratitude and make you feel like there's a point to your existence." She turned back to David.

"But they've never suffered, never wanted for anything. They can't understand pain, so they can't really care. So before his... enabling gets you hurt, let me be cruel to be kind. Drop this. Now. Go back to East Bloody Podunk and work at the general store."

"I've got nothing to go back to," David said. "No money to live on... or to buy a ticket with. The only way I can go is forward."

Her heart threatened to go out to the poor fool, so she yanked hard on its leash. "Rynyan was right. You are insane."

"You think I don't know how the galaxy looks at humans, Ms. Wing? That's the whole reason I'm out here. Because *somebody* has to be. Because we can't let ourselves be brainwashed into thinking the galaxy's right about us. Sure, they've all done wonderful things... but none of them are *us*."

"And what makes us so much better than anyone else?"

"We're not better. But we're *new*. We can come at the universe fresh, apply our unique way of thinking, maybe hit on something nobody else ever thought of.

"I'm not saying it's a sure thing. But I know humans can contribute something important to the galaxy. Why not this? And how will we ever know unless we try?"

"Well, you don't start small, I'll give you that."

"How can you not be excited at the possibility?" he continued, eyes gleaming. "I mean, you're a Hub scout! A pioneer, braving unknown frontiers, seeking out strange new worlds and new—"

"If you split an infinitive, I'm leaving," she told him. "You think this job is glamorous? Some big adventure you can tag along on? Let me tell you something. Space isn't empty. Space is *beyond* empty. At least 'empty' implies there's something there that can be filled. Space is nothing, with trace impurities.

"Now, imagine jumping randomly into nothing for a living. Imagine the odds of happening to materialize in range of one of those trace impurities, one that's interesting enough that people might want to come to it. Can you imagine that?" He thought it over, and she interrupted before he could speak. "I'll give you the answer: You can't. Whatever you're imagining, it's not even close.

"Now, imagine knowing that if you *do* eventually find a Hubpoint that's close to a star or planet, there's no way to know you won't emerge directly inside it and get an instant, no-fuss burial or cremation thrown in free with your death. Not that I'm complaining; that undercurrent of mortal terror before every dive helped relieve the monotony for the first year or so."

"And now?"

"Now it offers a ray of hope." He stared. "That's what being a Hub scout is, kid," she went on. "I don't do it for the adventure. I do it because I'm a human, and that means I'm desperate. I'd quit faster than a Hub dive if I got a better offer."

Rynyan leaned forward, leering. "That room in my mansion is still available for you."

"I said a *better* offer." She shuddered. "What is it with you? I'm not even your species."

"It is my duty as a Sosyryn to share my people's bounty with other species," he intoned. "If that includes sharing the wonders of Sosyryn sex, then I stand ready to serve."

"More like your own people are so decadent and dull that you have to look elsewhere for excitement. I'll stick to humans, thanks."

He shrugged. "Well, if you *want* to settle for males with only one penis…"

Mercifully, David got back on topic. "Look at it this way: your job won't be so boring if you have me along for company. I don't care if we find any interesting destinations—it's the jumps themselves I want to study." He smiled. "And it means your jumps will be accomplishing something even if they don't come out anywhere good."

"Except this crazy plan of yours isn't going to accomplish a bloody thing," she said.

He looked sad that he was unable to infect her with his enthusiasm. But he didn't give up trying. "Taking me along will accomplish one thing, at least. It'll get you paid. You can save up more toward getting a better job."

Nashira remained skeptical. "You can't even afford a ticket home. How're you gonna pay me?"

"Rynyan's agreed to fund the expedition."

She turned to Rynyan. "Really?"

"Absolutely. It sounds like a marvelous adventure. I'll be coming along, of course, to make sure my donation is put to good use."

Nashira quailed. The prospect of Rynyan's company almost outweighed that of Rynyan's money… but only almost. If Sosyryn got their kicks out of spreading their obscene wealth around on charity, who was she to refuse to take advantage of it? "Okay, Mr. LaMacchia."

"David."

She ignored it. "It's against my better judgment… but as long as I'm getting paid, you can come along… provided my supervisor okays it." Not that there was any chance Kred would go for it; he hated variations from procedure. But he wouldn't have any grounds to forbid it either. She just didn't want to seem too eager.

David took her hand and shook it ardently. "Thank you, Ms. Wing. When we crack the code of the Hub, I'll make sure the history wikis say only nice things about you."

Rynyan leaned across the table, putting a hand on her arm. "If all it takes to change your mind about an offer is money, my dear…"

A moment later, Rynyan began to understand pain.

"What's this about you taking on passengers, Wing?"

Nashira sighed. She should've known Mokak Vekredi would've found out about this. The mole-like Zeghryk may have been myopic in more ways than one, but he certainly seemed to hear about everything that went on in the Hubstation he managed. "Why, hello, Kred," she replied with feigned affection. "You're positively glowing today, dear. Pregnancy agrees with you."

The diminutive alien's night-adapted eyes darted away under their tinted goggles. "I don't know what you're referring to. I asked about these passengers. They're attempting to study Hub travel?"

"That's the idea. So when are the babies due?"

"I know of no babies," Vekredi insisted, ducking down

to hide his swollen belly behind his desk. Nashira stifled a laugh. Kred was so easy. Zeghryk were prolific breeders, hermaphrodites that could produce dozens of litters from a single mating. The boons of Hub contact had cured disease and conquered dangers, letting their population explode and forcing them to migrate off-world en masse. On learning that other races might feel threatened by their rampant growth, they'd made a decision typical of the officious Zeghryk mindset: by denying the problem existed, they could make it go away. They utterly refused to discuss the concept of sex or procreation with outsiders, insisted that they were all male, and denied ever being pregnant or raising children—even when they were visibly pregnant or surrounded by young, one or both of which they usually were. The xenosociologists had their theories for this strange behavior, but Nashira had her own theory, which was that Zeghryk were freaking idiots.

Which must be why they so often took jobs in middle management. "Your job is to search for profitable destinations," Vekredi went on. "Not to ferry tourists."

"Hub scouts take scientists along all the time. You know the regs, Kred. I'm not violating any procedures by bringing these guys along." She knew she'd have him there. He lacked the imagination to be comfortable with anything beyond clearly drawn procedure.

"Yes, but the Dosperhag want you to refuse this particular... expedition."

Nashira grimaced. *Unless it involves following direct orders from above.* "The Dospers don't own the Hub, Kred. Nobody does."

"It is in their territory."

"Only 'cause they moved their star system to keep it there."

"Exactly. The Dosperhag have an enormous investment in the Hub. They are entitled to... take an interest in its operation."

She shook her head. "You mean try to quash any attempt to figure out how the Hub works, just in case someone figures out how to build another one and take away their gravy train."

Vekredi blinked. "Their concerns run far beyond the import of meat-based sauces."

"Come on, Kred, they're being paranoid! Nobody's ever gonna crack the Hub."

"Of course not. But the Dosperhag feel that people should be discouraged from undertaking such futile efforts—possibly risking their lives for nothing."

She hoped she was right that Vekredi lacked the subtlety for that to be a veiled threat. "Look, this guy's just a kid with delusions of grandeur. He can barely find his sodding hotel room. The Dospers have nothing to worry about."

The little manager fidgeted. "I suppose not. However..." He leaned forward and spoke conspiratorially. "There is no procedure violated if his experiments... fail. And such failure would serve to... caution others against similar attempts."

Okay, so he did have a trace of subtlety after all. Not much, though. "No way, Kred. I'm not gonna sabotage this guy's equipment."

"What is your interest in defending him, Wing? Simply that he is of your species?"

He was really getting on her nerves now, so she reciprocated. "Yes, Kred. I'm madly in love with him. I'm going to spend the whole trip having wild, athletic sex with him." Vekredi cringed. Zeghryk didn't like discussing other species' sex lives either. "In fact, maybe I'll settle down with him and have lots and lots of babies. I bet you can give me all sorts of wonderful advice on mothering. Maybe your children can babysit for me!"

"They're not children!" Vekredi insisted by rote. "They're... small relatives. And none of this is pertinent."

"There's nothing pertinent about any of this, Kred! There's no point in sabotaging something that won't bloody work to begin with!"

The fidgeting increased. Kred was torn between two imperatives: following orders from his superiors and following his beloved procedures. She wondered if his head would explode. That would be fun to see. "There might be a point," he managed to say. "I know you are eager for promotion out of the scout position. A good performance review from me could open new doors for you, Ms. Wing."

For once, she had no comeback.

3

David counted himself lucky that Hubstation 3742 hosted its own Hub scout contingent. Apparently the scouting service was one of the ways that the junior civilizations affiliated with the Hubstation paid their way as members of the Network. But David would gladly have walked clear to the opposite side of the ring—the short way, through open space, if necessary—to have this opportunity. He beamed wide-eyed at the activity in the Scout Center as Hub scouts from a dozen species jogged, hopped, or tumbled through the staging area, some on their way from dorms to the locker room or the pilots' lounge, some heading for their Hubdiver ships, others returning from the docking bay to report their findings to the small, dark-goggled creature in the central office. These people were his heroes. But his attempts to strike up conversations with some of them earned only sullen glares or sharp dismissals. Deciding they must all be tightly focused on their work, David resolved not to distract them any further.

He trembled with excitement when Nashira Wing emerged from the locker room, looking thrillingly heroic in her Hubdiver jumpsuit, and then led David and Rynyan through the short corridor to her scout ship, the *Starship Entropy*. He felt a subtle resistance as he entered the scout, the pressure of the invisible nanofog that provided inertial damping and a semblance of gravity for the small ship's occupants. It did its job well; he felt only a mild push against the back of his seat as the launch rails accelerated the scout backward against the ring's rotation to cancel its angular momentum, then gave it a final radial push to send it in toward the Hub.

This time, David got to see the view. Once the *Entropy* cleared the rails and fell into open space, he gasped in awe. The sky was ablaze with stars and nebulosity in all directions, making the skies of Earth seem empty by comparison—but the Bulge itself filled nearly half the sky with an unbroken mass of yellow-white light. Against this magnificent backdrop lay the dozens of enormous ring habitats that surrounded the Hub concentrically in multiple planes, their rotations providing different gravity levels to accommodate the thousands of species participating in the Hub Network.

The *Entropy* was one of countless vessels shuttling between the Hubstation rings and the heavily armored Shell that encased the Hub, the light from their various drive sinks and exhausts creating a multicolored light show rivaling the galactic splendor beyond. It looked like freeway gridlock on Earth, except in three dimensions and less cluttered; the lethally hot plasma exhaust from fusion engines tended to discourage tailgating.

But Hub scouts were usually given priority, since there were simply so many untried Hub vectors remaining to test. The *Entropy* was able to soar past the gridlock on a reserved vector and was soon passing through a hatch in the Shell. "That's no moon, it's a space station," David quipped, but Nashira ignored him.

As they passed through the intricate array of launchers and scanners inside the Shell, David was finally able to look upon the Hub itself. It was less impressive-looking than he'd expected: just an odd pucker in the center of the Shell, faintly glowing with the trace energy that seeped through from literally every point within the galactic halo, but oddly difficult to focus his eyes on.

But as the *Entropy* took its place on the launch rail and was shunted around the curve of the Shell toward its dive trajectory, David remembered just how impressive the Hub really was. "This is so cool," he said. "Here we are, about to go someplace no human or Sosyryn has ever been in the history of the universe."

"Yep," Nashira said. "Hey, you did remember to update your will, right?" David swallowed, suddenly remembering what Nashira had said about the risks of her job. She cackled at his expression. "Now that's the Hub scout spirit. Nice knowin' ya, fuckers!" she cried as the *Entropy* was launched from the rail and dove into the Hub. David missed the transition because his eyes were squeezed shut.

After a few moments, he realized he wasn't dead, and dared to open them again—only to gasp at the vista that spread before him on the cockpit's wraparound display wall. Out there, just beyond the ship's nose, the whole expanse of the Milky Way spread out before him, its two major spiral arms and central bar clearly delineated. Off to the side, both Magellanic Clouds were visible, two small, irregular clumps of light with a faint streamer barely detectable between them, even with the display wall's amplification. He looked to the other side and saw a spray of red-orange stars, a globular cluster a few thousand parsecs off their starboard bow.

"Wow," he finally said. "Wow. There, you see, Nashira? Our very first dive, and we get something... this beautiful. What are the odds of that?"

She rolled her eyes. "Oh, about four thousand, nine hundred and ninety-nine in five thousand. Dives can take you anywhere inside the halo, and the galaxies make up a fiftieth of a percent of that by volume. I see views like this every bloody day, and so do the tourists who go to the hundreds of destinations with views just like this. Destinations that actually have nearby stars to support the tour facilities. Here, we'd be lucky to find a speck of dust within a parsec."

As David's face fell, Nashira worked the controls. "Now let's get back before we lose the beam."

He put his hand on her arm. "Wait. Can't we just stay here a little longer? It's my first time."

"And it's my first time today. I've got a lot of vectors left to test."

"Please? Come on, can't you remember what it was like the first time you saw this?"

She sighed. "All right, I guess there's no harm."

"Uhh, we can call for pickup after the beam's shut down, right?"

"Long as we've got the 'lopes."

David kept drinking in the sight until the laser beam that "held the door open" along their Hub vector shut down, about four minutes after the dive. When the Dosperhag had first stumbled upon the Hub sixteen millennia ago, they had lost many probes and ships to one-way interstellar journeys before discovering the beam effect. That simple discovery had made the Hub viable for interstellar travel and begun bringing the galaxy together. As a result, the Dosperhag had become one of the most prosperous and influential races in the galaxy—although their low-gravity, metal-poor biology limited their ability to visit other worlds, so they were content to share the burden of managing the Hub with others. David cast a glance back at his instruments, hoping they would bring about another simple revolution—for the benefit of all, but in the name of humanity.

Nashira caught his glance. "Okay, I might as well ask—what's this big theory of yours for how the Hub works?"

He smiled at her interest, however marginal it sounded. "Well, I got the idea from a twentieth-century physicist called Richard Feynman. He thought that every particle in the universe was really the same particle, bouncing back and forth endlessly through space and time. I think he was onto something. I'm theorizing that every particle in the universe is just a cross-section of one great big cosmic string... and the Hub is a sort of tangle where all the paths intersect. The Hub vectors are the paths the strings take. So if I can identify the string signatures and how they intersect, we'll be able to predict where a Hub vector comes out!"

Nashira stared at him blankly until David said, "Was I clear enough? Do you need something explained?"

After another moment, she turned to Rynyan in the back. "Rynyan, I owe you an apology. For once, you were right. You've found yourself a grade-A lunatic."

Rynyan preened. "I bring you nothing but the best, my pet."

"It just sounds crazy to you because it's not accepted by the galaxy," David told her. "But that's exactly the kind of new idea we need to try!"

"Forget it. I'm just the driver. You play with your gadgets

all you want, doesn't matter to me. Whatever happens with that stuff, it's not my problem."

David chuckled. "You make it sound like something bad's going to happen. What could go wrong?"

"Nothing. Never mind." Nashira cleared her throat and headed back to the communication shack. "I'm calling for retrieval."

David hastened to follow. "Ooh, I want to watch. I've never seen a quantelope."

A quantelope was a small, rabbit-like creature with purple fur and two small horns on its head. And the whole of galactic civilization rested upon its tiny shoulders. The Hub allowed instantaneous travel, but the blanket energy leakage obscured any radio traffic. The only way to communicate with the Hub from a distance, whether to confirm a viable Hubpoint or to request a beam for a return trip, was by talking to a quantelope. Somehow, in the ultra-cold environs of their homeworld, these ammonia-based animals had evolved with Bose-Einstein condensates in their bloodstreams, allowing their brains to become quantum-entangled with those of their kith and kin. A little gengineering had turned them into quantum radios, able to parrot anything heard by one of their entanglemates. Which made them dandy for interstellar communication but unwise to keep as pets in one's bedroom.

David was torn between staring in awe and giggling as the tiny, adorable beastie stared up out of its cryotank and intoned in a deep voice, "You're overdue, *Entropy*. Anything to report?"

"False alarm," Nashira said, and asked for a beam. Moments later, as they returned to the cockpit, a spot of laser light appeared in the middle of nowhere, Hubpoint distortion scattering enough of its light to make it visible from any direction. Nashira piloted the *Entropy* until it aligned with the beam and rode it back through the Hub.

"Do us both a favor," Nashira said once they were in the Shell again. "Get off now and take Don Wannabe here with you. You're not going to find anything."

"We've barely even started," David said. "And I, for one, would love to see our galaxy from a few dozen more angles."

She turned to David's backer. "How about you, Rynyan? We've been doing this for nearly fifteen minutes. We must have exceeded your attention span by now."

"I am never bored so long as I have your beauty to gaze upon," he said. "Though honestly, that jumpsuit doesn't let me gaze upon nearly enough of your beauty. I'll buy you some Earth lingerie to wear for me tomorrow."

Nashira spun the ship around sharply to re-dock on the launch rail, sending Rynyan into the bulkhead. "Ooh, I love it when you get physical," he said.

"Last chance to get off, save us all some grief," she told David.

"I don't give up that easy," he replied. "Let's dive."

The second dive was on the same trajectory as before, but a centimeter per second faster. They came out a good hundred kiloparsecs from where they'd been, this time seeing the Milky Way edge-on from the other side. Over the next few dozen jumps, David certainly got his wish to see his home galaxy—and the various satellites and clusters that shared its dark-matter halo—from every possible angle.

On the second day, Rynyan's generous donation of lingerie items was jettisoned eight thousand parsecs beyond the Canis Major Dwarf galaxy. On the third day, they actually materialized inside the Virgo Stellar Stream, the remnant of a dwarf spheroidal galaxy being torn apart as it slowly merged with the Milky Way's disk. Despite his fascination with the extragalactic vistas, David was somewhat relieved to see a starry sky, even a sparse one like this. "I'm picking up energy readings," Nashira reported. "Looks like radar transmissions."

David perked up. "A new species? First contact?"

Her eyes were wide as she studied the readings, narrowing in on the source. "Maybe. If we're lucky…"

"I bet you get a huge bonus for this!"

"Wouldn't suck…"

After a moment, she slumped. Then she socked David in the shoulder, hard. "Damn you! You sodding moron, trying to get my hopes up!"

"What is it? No aliens?"

"Oh, there are aliens, all right! Great big sodding technical civilization, colonies all over their system."

"Then what—"

"*They're eight light-years away*, that's what! We can't go there! We can't make contact! This is even worse than finding nothing! Do you get now why I hate this job?"

"Hey, it's not a total loss. I'm sure they'll want to set up a science outpost here to study them."

"Oh, great, scientists. No tourism, no trade. I'll be able to buy new shoes with my bonus." She grimaced. "And now I have to fall further behind schedule so I can collect preliminary readings. A little present for the grandkids I'm never gonna have at this rate."

"Hey, doing science. That sounds exciting."

"You want to do science? You want to help?"

"Do I!"

She pointed. "Push that button."

He did so. "Now what?"

"That's it. It's done. The ship's taking readings. What do you think, I have xenology degrees? I'm a bloody pilot." She crossed her arms. "Nothing to do now but sit and wait."

She went back to get a sandwich. David heard Rynyan moving to intercept her. "If you'd like a way to pass the time, I've been studying this book called the *Kama Sutra*. I think its proposals would be very adaptable to a merging of our species."

"You remember David's theory, Rynyan? About how the particles in all our bodies are really the same particle looping back on itself?"

"Yes," he replied, nonplussed.

"Well, if he's right, then if you want to have sex with me... you can just go fuck yourself."

"These are acceptable results," Vekredi told Nashira as he reviewed her reports. "I'll forward them to Research for eventual follow-up. The size of your bonus will be contingent on how these results pan out."

Nashira declined to hold her breath. It was a big galaxy, plus eight small galaxies, and there was already plenty to keep the universities and research centers of the Network worlds busy for centuries. If she were lucky, she might see the bonus before she retired. If she lived that long.

"Meanwhile, I trust Mr. LaMacchia has made no progress?"

"Of course not, Kred."

He peered at her through his goggles. "Then you have taken action to… neutralize his equipment?"

"His equipment is off-the-shelf junk, and he barely knows how to use it. Even if there were something to find, I'm not gonna bother sabotaging something that has no chance of finding it. I don't kick people when they're already down for the count. Not worth the pain in my toes."

"Very well," Vekredi said after a moment. "Since your position is clear, the subject will not be raised with you again."

"It better not be." She didn't tell him how close she'd come to sabotaging David's equipment anyway. That bonus would have done her some real good, even if it had been for a pointless act. But if she'd let Kred and his bosses use her that way once, she'd never be free of them.

And maybe, on some level, she didn't like the idea of betraying David LaMacchia. Not that she was getting sentimental; if she'd felt it was in her best interests to screw him over, she would've screwed him over and had no trouble living with it. But she was just a little bit glad she didn't have to.

4

They soon settled into a daily routine, with David improvising new scan techniques with his instruments while Rynyan "supervised" and flirted and Nashira tried her best to ignore them both. Each morning she advised them to give up and leave her to her sullen solitude, and each morning they climbed aboard with unrelenting enthusiasm.

"I don't believe you're really that cynical about space," David insisted one morning. Smiling, he gestured toward his eye. "I looked up your name. Nashira's a star in Capricorn—and its name means 'bringer of good news.' And you're, what, early thirties? I bet you were conceived just after Hub contact, when people were so excited about the stars opening up to us. Your parents must've wanted—"

"Stop."

"But I just—"

She grabbed the front of his shirt and pulled his face close to hers. "Just stop. Say one more word about my parents and you'll end up where my lingerie went." His eyes goggled at her. She winced. "I mean, where Rynyan's lingerie—" She shoved him back. "Just shut up!"

At least David looked more embarrassed than she felt. *Please tell me that wasn't a Freudian slip. And by 'slip' I don't mean—oh, shut up.* Fortunately Rynyan hadn't heard the remark, and David quickly forgot about it as his studies preoccupied him.

But after a week in which none of the three made any progress toward their respective goals, David was beginning to think a change of tack was needed. "We need to go through the Hub as slowly as possible," he told Nashira. "Just drift into it.

Maybe a slower passage will get me better readings."

"The jump's instantaneous," Nashira said.

"But it can't be. The front of the ship enters the Hub before the back does. There has to be some kind of transition."

"The controllers won't like it. A slow dive means delays for other ships."

David turned to the Sosyryn. "Rynyan?"

"Not to worry. I'm wiring the bribes into their accounts as we speak."

And so, thanks to Sosyryn generosity, one controller was able to buy a lavish anniversary meal for each of his six spouses, another was able to decorate her hothouse-dwelling with the finest K'slien pornographic topiaries, and Nashira was able to read insulting and threatening instant messages from a dozen fellow pilots before the *Starship Entropy* finally crept through the Hub.

She was still composing suitably scathing replies when they reached the other side, hoping to provoke a good brawl in the pilots' lounge later on and get enough bones broken to justify a medical leave. So she ignored David's gasp of amazement. Then she ignored Rynyan's gasp of amazement.

Then Rynyan grabbed her head from behind and tilted it up to the viewing wall. And she gasped in amazement.

"I've never seen anything like that," David said.

"Neither have I," Rynyan said, "and I'm not even a backwater hick."

"I don't know if anyone has," Nashira said.

What they saw, so the *Entropy* computer told them after digesting a few minutes of scans, was a red giant star a few AUs in front of them. But not just any red giant. This star had not one or two, but four hot Jovians in close orbits around it. All four had been engulfed by the star's expanding atmosphere as it swelled past its main-sequence confines. But they had not been fully vaporized, for they were large, and the extremely hot hydrogen around them was also extremely tenuous. Rather, they had carved out gaps in the vast hydrogen cloud, bulldozing their orbital paths clear. Their gravity had concentrated the star's hydrogen into the zones between their orbits, confining it against the outward push of the stellar wind from the white-hot, dying core. Friction with the stellar atmosphere had eroded their own atmospheres, which had coursed behind the planets like cometary tails and been blown outward to mingle with the confined hydrogen in between them, spiking it with trace amounts of ammonia, methane, ice crystals, hydrocarbons, and organic compounds.

In short, the newly dead white dwarf was surrounded by a system of immense, multicolored rings, so vast that the Jovian planets functioned as shepherd moons. These rings were encased within the tenuous remains of the red giant's outer atmosphere, minus the layers that had already sloughed off to begin forming a planetary nebula around it, nested shells encasing the nested rings.

"This is the most beautiful thing I've ever seen," David said.

"The hell with that—this is gonna make me rich!" Nashira replied with glee. "Oh, we'd better get back so I can stake a claim on this place! Wing's Rings, they'll call it!"

"You can do that?" Rynyan asked.

"If I'm quick about it. If I can do an end run, get the paperwork done in my name before I have to report this to Kred. I'll still have a ton of debt to work off, but eventually I should be able to get out of this shitty job and rub my success in their faces and assorted sensory clusters. One last scan for parallax readings, and then we go back!"

"Whoa, what's your hurry?" David asked. "Come on, Nashira, look at it! You've found something incredibly beautiful, something that nobody has ever seen before. How can you not be thrilled by this? How can you not give yourself a little time to be moved by it?"

She glared at him. "You're right. This is an amazing place. It's gorgeous. Anyone would give a fortune to retire here. *And I can never see it again.* That's a Hub scout's life, understand? We try the new vectors, the ones nobody's been to before. Well, we've been here now, and that means I'm not coming back. So where's the percentage in letting myself give a damn about it, except as a way of maybe someday getting out of this life?"

He was nonplussed. "But… if you did get out, you could still come back."

"If I'm lucky," she told him, reality setting back in. "If nothing else goes wrong. If I don't materialize inside a brown dwarf tomorrow. That's my life, kid."

David was quiet for a time. "I'm really sorry," he said, and it sounded like pity, so she hated him for it.

She spent a few minutes ignoring him, studying the new set of scans to make sure there was nothing here to jinx her find. Once she was satisfied, she jumped out of her chair and headed to the comm shack, pushing past Rynyan, who was loitering in the hatchway and clearly relishing the close contact. "I'm calling for the beam. Sooner you two dreamers are out of my hair, the better." *And out of my head.*

A few moments later, she screamed. "What is it?" David cried, rushing in after her with Rynyan behind him. She just pointed and let them see for themselves:

The quantelopes were dead.

A quick investigation showed that the cryotank's supposedly failure-proof systems had failed. The quantelopes had boiled alive well before reaching room temperature. "Well!" Rynyan declared. "I shall certainly complain to the manufacturer when we get back."

"When we get *back?!*" Nashira cried. "How exactly do we *do* that? We have no way of contacting the Hub!"

"Won't they send a ship to find us when we don't report in?" David asked.

"In about five years, maybe. For all they know, we're inside a planet or got caught in a war or a supernova wavefront. They'll give it time for the danger to move past the Hubpoint."

"Oh." He paused. "Well, we'll have to figure something out ourselves, then."

"Don't you get it?! We're *dead!* There's nowhere habitable in this system. The ship's got less than a week's supplies for three. God, it'd be better if we'd come out right inside the bloody star, been flash-vaporized."

She went back to the cockpit and took her seat, tempted to fire up the drive and fly the *Entropy* into the star. Instead, she just clunked her head down on the console and wrapped her arms around it. *I never thought I'd go this way. I thought I'd never even know I'd died.* She damned the universe for getting her hopes up just before it killed her.

She felt a hand on her shoulder—a human one, at least. "Maybe there's another way," David said. "Maybe the scans I took can let us figure out a way back, or at least a way to contact the Hub."

"Stop deluding yourself, kid. You… are going… to fucking… die."

He sat down beside her. "I don't think it's deluded to go on trying. If you try, at least you have a chance. If you don't try, you have none.

"That's the whole point of what you do, Nashira. It's why I admire you so much. Your job, it's all about playing the long odds, risking it all to find things you have only the tiniest chance of finding. The fact that you do this job at all tells me that there must be a part of you that believes in hope."

"Hope just sets you up for disappointment, David."

"I don't believe in disappointment," Rynyan said. "Just delayed gratification. We'll be home by dinnertime." He rubbed his belly. "That reminds me, I need a snack."

"Go ahead," Nashira told him. "No point in rationing our food anyway."

"Nashira…"

"Don't, David. You just go play with your toys until you figure out we're buggered."

He spent a few hours with his instruments before growling in frustration. "Let me guess," Nashira said.

"It's not hopeless," he insisted. "Just difficult."

"There's nothing there."

"There's some data… I just have to figure it out."

"Random noise."

"I'm not giving up. At least…" He sighed. "At least it's something to keep me occupied if…"

"So you're finally starting to admit it."

He returned to his seat next to hers. "Okay. Maybe we are going to die here."

She stared. "How can you be so calm about it?"

"Are you kidding?" He gestured to the display. "I got to see *that*."

"You're not disappointed that you'll never get to crack the Hub and make the galaxy sit up and notice humanity?"

"At least I tried. I set a goal for myself, a *big* goal. Something more than just working a nine-to-five and watching the vidnet. That's not enough of a life anymore, not when there's a whole universe for us to reach for. I know a lot of people back home who dream of coming out here. But they'll never actually do it. Because they're not stupid or crazy enough to risk everything to try it. But I was. I was stupid. I was crazy. And so I really *tried*. And I made it out here. Maybe I'm going to die, but at least I actually *lived* first." He turned back to admire the rings. "Just look at it, Nashira. We get to see something nobody else has ever seen. And it's all ours, for the rest of our lives. That's not so bad a way to go, is it?"

Nashira looked into his eyes for a while. Then she turned to the display and really *saw* the rings for the first time.

After a while, the rings blurred, and she realized she was crying. In wonder. "It really is beautiful."

"It's an amazing universe," David said.

"Yeah... I guess sometimes it is." She found herself looking into his eyes again... and not wanting to look away. She felt herself moving closer to him, closer...

And then the proximity alert went off. Nashira spun back to the console in bewilderment. "What? There—there's a ship coming! It just came through the Hub! We're saved!"

"Well, it's about time they got here," Rynyan spoke up. "The snacks on this ship aren't very good."

Nashira heard something more than his usual cluelessness in his voice. She turned to face him. "'They' who?"

"Oh, just some friends of mine. Business partners, really. They're here to secure my claim."

She stood. *"Your* claim?"

He grinned and gestured toward the glorious vista beyond. "Welcome to Rynyan's Rings. I'm going to donate them as a federal park, so the entire Network can benefit from them!"

"You—you! You—when the hell did you... How did you...?"

"Oh, I called them hours ago! While you were doing the parallax scan. The quantelopes were fine when I used them. Well, alive, at least. Rather sluggish, come to think of—"

"You bastard!" She pinned him against the bulkhead. "You come aboard *my* ship and you have the gall to jump *my* claim?!"

"I prefer to think of it as saving your life. Which I'm sure you'll agree is a *much* more generous act than letting you have the claim to the Rings. Along with my donation of the Rings themselves, I'll be the envy of all Rysos come tallying season!"

"Saving my—you didn't even know we'd be in danger when you made that call!"

"The intent doesn't matter," he said with the serene smile of the *bodhisattva* who'd eaten the canary. "The meaning lies in the gift itself."

5

"The failure of the cryotank is being investigated," Vekredi told them upon their return to Hubstation 3742. "Naturally the reliability of our quantelope communication is of the highest priority to us. But I hope this incident has driven home to you, Mister LaMacchia, that Hub scout missions are intrinsically dangerous. If you continue your... researches in this vein, the Hub management cannot be held liable for the consequences. Do you understand me, sir?"

"Yes, thanks," David said. "Your translator's working fine."

Vekredi nodded in satisfaction and waddled away. Once he was out of earshot, Nashira punched David in the shoulder. "Don't you get it, kid? Translated or not, that was a threat. No way that tank just happened to fail. It was sabotaged."

His eyes widened. "Are you sure?"

"I can't prove it, but I know it. The Dospers wanted me to sabotage your equipment, but I refused. So they had someone sabotage my ship instead."

"Why would they do that?"

"Because they don't want to lose their monopoly on interstellar travel! If you keep digging, David, they'll keep trying to stop you."

"Oh my God," he said. Then he grinned. "This is great!"

"It's great that they tried to kill us?"

"Don't you get it, Nashira? Thousands of species have studied the Hub and found nothing. If the Dosperhag are afraid of what I'm doing ... it means they must think there's a chance that I can find something. A chance that humans—insignificant, irrelevant humans—can offer the galaxy something that nobody else can.

"And you know what that means?"

"It means," Rynyan said thoughtfully, "that maybe there is an answer after all. One the Dosperhag have been covering up. You might actually be sane after all." He slumped. "Aww."

"More than that," David said. "It means—"

Nashira sighed, troubled that she was beginning to understand how he thought. "It means you can't give up now. That you're gonna keep trying to show the galaxy what humanity can do."

"That's right." He shrugged. "Maybe I won't keep studying Hub travel—not openly, anyway. I'm not *that* stupid." He winked. "But there have got to be other things humans have to offer the galaxy. And I'm going to find them, no matter how long it takes. Just like you're gonna find another special place someday, no matter how long it takes."

"And just as I," said Rynyan, "will find a way to share the wonders of Sosyryn sex with Nashira, no matter how—"

"Not happening, Goldilocks," she told him absently before turning back to David. "You're gonna get yourself in so many kinds of trouble."

"Then it's a good thing I have Rynyan to help me out."

"Like I said: you're gonna get in so many kinds of trouble." She sighed again, knowing she was going to have to keep an eye on the kid until he got a better feel for the big, bad galaxy. If only because she shuddered to think what would happen to humanity's reputation with David and Rynyan carrying the torch.

But maybe, she thought as she studied David's eyes and infectious smile, she had one or two other reasons to care what happened to him. Maybe he'd reminded her what it felt like to care.

So she'd have to stick close until she figured out whether to thank him or take revenge.

COME VISIT BEAUTIFUL RYNYAN'S RINGS

NEWEST WONDER OF THE GREATER GALAXY!

The Rynyan Zynara Charitable Trust is proud to announce the grand opening of Rynyan's Rings, the most spectacular stellar remnant of the modern era. Even if you've lived for a thousand years and traveled across the entire Network, you've never seen a sight like this! Four close-orbiting giant planets carve the expelled atmosphere of this dying star into the vastest, most beautiful ring system you've ever seen! Our scientists say it will only last for six millennia, so see it while you can!

Rynyan's Rings were discovered on Network Date 23,409/7778-12.Orange during a research expedition funded and led by noted philanthropist Rynyan Zynara ad Surynyyyyyy'a. Come visit and hear the harrowing story of how the discovery almost ended in disaster thanks to poor quantelope maintenance by the expedition's junior-species pilot. Rynyan's quick thinking in summoning a rescue party before the quantelope tank failed not only saved the lives of the expedition members, but brought the wonder of Rynyan's Rings to the greater galaxy—and now to you!

Rynyan's Rings can be admired from the comfort of the luxurious Rynyan Station, a lavishly appointed resort positioned conveniently near the Hubpoint. Perfect for a one-of-a-kind vacation with your family, commune-pod, or memetic affiliates... or an unforgettable rendezvous with that special someone(s). Experience our low-gravity spa... our sun rooms for every solar spectrum... our hyperdimensional play palace for children, budlings, and rejuvenants ... our full-immersion sensory-emotive theater... and our fully accredited staff of intimate pleasure providers of all sex and gender categories, both biological and cybernetic. And don't forget to admire the Rings themselves while you're here! Our live shuttle tours and telepresence probes will let you admire the Rings and their shepherd worlds up close, a majestic experience that you'll remember for the rest of your life and well into whatever life continuation you select *[complete memory reboots excluded]*!

Rynyan Station offers delights for every taste, a gift for all Hub Network denizens courtesy of the Rynyan Zynara Charitable Trust. Rynyan donated it all for you, and he's sure the majesty of the Rings and the luxuries of Rynyan Station will inspire visitors to follow his lead and donate generously in turn!

Rynyan's Rings are located at Hub vector θ 136.56134977º/φ 54.35170653º/v 0.48 m/s. It's a slow dive, but it's worth the wait! Book your vacation now!

HOME IS WHERE THE HUB IS

1

Nashira Wing fidgeted with the straps of her slinky dress as she signaled at the door of Suite 47. She practically jumped out of said dress when the door opened and a huge, slavering carnivore thrust out its head. "Are you room service?" it said. "About time. I'm starving." Several snake-tongue tentacles darted out to sniff at her limbs. "Are the exposed parts the ones that will grow back? Don't worry, my venom anesthetizes you."

"Ahh, no," Nashira said, regaining her aplomb. She stared down banal and pointless death every day; at least the sight of a huge hyperdentate mouth got the adrenaline flowing a bit. "Sorry, I must've hit the wrong button. I want Room 4."

The beast—more properly, the Qhpong—reared its head and all its tongues back. "Oh, you must be David's mating partner! Of course, I should've recognized the species. Hard to tell with your scent masked like that."

"Yeah, we're funny that way."

The Qhpong looked her over again, with its eyes this time. "And so many exposed parts, too. A pity. But never mind. I like that David. Such a polite fellow. And he smells delicious. You're a lucky female."

"I am? Um. Sure. Yes, I am."

The Qhpong went back inside, muttering about calling room service and threatening to eat some of their parts without anesthesia. Nashira again hit the door signal, hoping that this time it would connect her to the right facet of the tesseract-shaped suite within. By now, thanks to the inept maintenance in this fleabag hotel, virtually all of the suite's other occupants had become aware of her frequent visits to David LaMacchia, and they'd become an object of gossip around Hubstation 3742. David liked it that way, but Nashira could do without the embarrassment.

This time, the dimensional interface worked properly and David answered. "Oh, great, you're here!" The young, sandy-haired American ushered her in quickly, shut the door, and activated the small cubic room's privacy field. His eyes went straight to her purse. "Is that it?"

Nashira glared. "What? No comment about the dress?"

"What? Oh, you look gorgeous," he said absently. "Now, come on, let me see the module."

Gorgeous? Nashira was too nonplussed to resist as David took the purse and rummaged through it, retrieving the gravitational sensor module she'd been smuggling aboard her Hubdiver ship for the past week. After a moment, she shook it off. Why should she care whether this feckless rube noticed her? She could do better any day of the week. Or she could if her arrangement with David didn't require the pretense that their private meetings were of a personal nature. She sighed. *What a waste of good perfume.*

Besides, she'd been the one who'd warned David against trying any funny stuff when he'd first proposed this arrangement a month ago. It had taken him so long to realize what she was concerned about that she'd questioned whether he even liked women. "Oh, I like most everybody," he'd assured her breezily.

"I mean—"

"I know what you mean," he'd replied with an abashed smile. "I'm not that... experienced... with either guys or girls, but I like them both just fine. Not to worry, though, Nashira—I promise I'll be the perfect gentleman with you. This is too important to me to mess up."

And the ensuing weeks had borne that out. Despite all the time she'd spent alone with David in these close quarters, all he'd cared about had been his quest to crack the secrets of the Hub and thereby prove humanity's worth to interstellar civilization. And that added up to the most boring set of late nights she'd ever spent in a sexy dress. Not that Nashira couldn't sympathize with his goals; if it were possible to predict which entry vector would lead to which point in the greater galaxy, she would no longer have to risk her life testing Hub vectors at random. But what David saw as the fresh, unbiased perspective of a new, young species, Nashira saw only as terminal cluelessness.

And even David's optimism could only take him so far. After a while, he groaned, tossing the instruments aside. "Still nothing."

"Don't tell me that still surprises you," Nashira said. "I've made more slow dives this month than a base jumper on Phobos, but the transition's still as good as instantaneous. And even if it weren't, the Hub leaks signal from every radiating body within a hundred kiloparsecs. There's no way to tease any data out of that wall-to-wall white noise. What, you think you're the first person to try it this way in sixteen thousand years?"

"Nashira, if there were no chance, we wouldn't have to put on this act. The fact that the Dosperhag want to stop us means there must be a way."

"You mean the fact they tried to bloody kill us."

Nashira was startled by a chime at the door. "Oh, get that, will you?" David asked. "That'll be Rynyan."

"Rynyan!" Nashira raced to the entrance and yanked the Sosyryn inside, looking around furtively. "What are you doing here?" she hissed as she shut the door.

The tawny Sosyryn absently preened his feathery mane. "David invited me."

"What?! Nobody saw you, did they?"

"Oh, I just had a charming conversation with the Qhpong in Room 5. Don't worry, I didn't blow our cover; I told her I was here for a threesome."

Nashira winced, cursing under her breath in Cantonese. Putting up with David was manageable, but it meant putting up with Rynyan as well. Nashira didn't mind Rynyan's generous bribes for smuggling David's equipment, but she could do without his supercilious attitude and his relentless come-ons—and she wasn't about to forgive him for jumping the claim on the greatest find of her career. Only the fact that he'd inadvertently saved her life in the process kept her from ending his. Having no concept of failure or deprivation, though, Rynyan kept on cheerfully flirting no matter how often she shot him down. At least David's inability to accept failure was due to good old human self-delusion... though he would call it hope.

Rynyan looked her over. "And she was right, you do look good enough to eat. What do you say we make me an honest Sosyryn? Although I could live with telling a small lie, if you'd rather we just had a twosome. Either way, I do need accurate details to post on my daily journal."

Nashira stifled a scream, causing David to look up in alarm. "That's it! Risking my arse is one thing, but my reputation can't take any more of this!" She stormed to the door. "No more fake trysts. If you two want to scan the Hub anymore, you'll just have to come on a dive and take your bloody chances along with me."

Perversely, predictably, David grinned at the prospect, leaping off the bed. "Great! I've been dying to get back into space! Can we go tomorrow?"

She should've known counting on David's sanity was a mistake. "If you don't mind risking instant and horrible deaths, sure."

He shrugged. "You told me you scan for sabotage before every dive session now."

"There may be other ways they can screw us."

"Here at the Hub, with so many witnesses, they wouldn't dare. And on the other end, they can't do anything." He smiled and took her hands. "Besides... I trust you to take good care of us."

Her heart raced, and she cursed herself. How did he always manage to get through her armor? She turned to Rynyan. "Don't tell me—you're coming along too. Even though we could die."

"Oh, relax," Rynyan replied glibly. "Death is something that happens to *other* people."

The call from Dosp came at the worst possible moment for Mokak Vekredi. Had it been any other caller, he would have told them he was on vacation. But his job, and thus the survival of his large and growing family (growing at this very moment), depended on pleasing his superiors. So he had his companions (he'd trained himself not to think of them as his children, lest he slip up and confess the relationship in public) help him over to the quantelope tank and then strive to conduct the ongoing operation as silently as possible—though Vekredi himself was the one who would normally make the most noise. "I'm—I'm here, Morjepas," he managed to get out, keeping his gasps to a minimum.

The quantelope turned its adorable little stubby-horned face toward Vekredi and spoke in a reedy Dosperhag voice, carried instantaneously across the light-hours from Dosp by the quantum link binding this 'lope to its entanglemate in Morjepas's office. "Vekredi, are you all right?"

"Per-perfectly! *Aah!*" He was grateful the small purple creatures could only mimic the sounds their entanglemates heard and not reproduce the sights. "There's... *unh*... nothing going on here! Nnn*yaah!*"

"You're giving birth, aren't you?"

"Why, sir!" he got out between grunts. "I have no comprehension... what you mean. I'm simply doing... paperwork." The first baby came free and began emitting peeping cries. "Oh, pardon me, that's a... call I need to put on hold." He gestured frantically at one of his companions to take the baby into the other room.

"Oh, please," Morjepas said through the 'lope. "Everyone knows Zeghryk are prolific breeders. You're not fooling anyone."

"Was there... some specific reason you... needed me, Morjepas?"

"It can wait a few hours."

"No, really ... I'm not doing ... anything important."

The quantelope sighed. "Very well, have it your way. It's about your report that the human LaMacchia is taking dives with Scout Wing again."

"Yes... that is correct."

"You're permitting this?"

"I have no... grounds for denying it. *Aaah!*" The second baby was reluctant to come out. Or maybe Vekredi was just too tense. This was an extremely private thing, only for Zeghryk. Even the scrutiny of a quantelope was deeply humiliating.

"That's true," Morjepas said after a moment. "I don't suppose there's any chance their relationship is actually sexual?"

Vekredi's cringe had nothing to do with his labor pains. What was private for Zeghryk should be private for everyone, particularly for such disgustingly non-hermaphroditic creatures as humans. "I have no opinion."

"Well, we're fairly certain it's a cover for his continued investigations of the Hub. The dimensional walls in his hotel suite are thin, and our agent there has heard no sounds consistent with human copulation."

At this rate, Vekredi's cringe muscles would be as sore as... certain others. "Stipulated! Stipulated. What do you propose we do to deter them?"

"Now, Vekredi, you know that the Dosperhag officially have no objection to Hub research."

"Of course."

"So it has to look like an accident."

Vekredi winced, for more reasons than one. He imagined the second baby was looking at him sullenly as another companion took it away. He hoped this call would end soon so he could begin nursing. "What do you have in mind?"

"The next time Scout Wing takes LaMacchia on a dive, assign her to the following Hub vector." The quantelope recited a string of numbers. Vekredi called them up from his memory implant and reviewed the information.

"But Morjepas... that's a dormant vector! Two consecutive scouts disappeared there. The last was only... twelve years ago." If the danger had persisted for the five years between scouts, it was doubtful the Hubpoint had drifted away from it since then. Procedure dictated waiting at least twenty years before a third attempt.

"Vekredi, you do understand the point of this exercise, don't you?"

With a sigh, Vekredi said, "Yes, Morjepas. I'll assign Scout Wing the vector."

"I'm sorry about this, Mokak. Are you fond of Scout Wing?"

Vekredi pondered the question. "Actually, no." The thought cheered him. Having to replace a Hubdiver ship and train a new scout would be a hassle. Such losses were part of the business, but it clashed with his orderly administrative impulses to bring them on deliberately. But being spared Nashira Wing's unruly, disrespectful manner and her constant taunts about his alleged parenthood (he sighed as the third baby finally came out—only five more to go!) would be a definite consolation.

Humans. Nothing but trouble, the lot of them. And more of them keep infesting my nice orderly Hubstation. They breed like vermin, that's the problem. He shuddered as the fourth baby made its way down the birth canal.

2

It was a long way from Hubstation 3742 to the Shell. The inner habitat rings were reserved for the more prominent or ancient species within the Hub Network, while junior worlds like Earth got relegated to the more remote, crowded outer rings. A Hub scout like Nashira got priority clearance, but still it took a good twenty minutes for the *Starship Entropy* to reach the Shell. David didn't mind, since it gave him plenty of time to drink in the gorgeous view of the galaxy's Central Bulge filling half the sky. He counted himself lucky that the Magellanic Clouds offset the center of mass of the overall galactic system away from the Milky Way's center. What if every large galaxy had a Hub, but most of them were lost inside their core black holes?

Wouldn't be much of a view then, I guess.

The view within the Shell was almost as spectacular, a kilometers-wide spherical space filled with the elaborate tracks and launch rails that propelled ships on their finely calibrated dive vectors into the Hub itself at the center. David continued to be amazed at the precision of the Shell's technology, necessary since the tiniest error in angle or velocity could send a ship to the wrong galaxy altogether; but he was glad he didn't need it. His mission—well, Nashira's mission, with him tagging along—was to deliberately take those unknown vectors that others tried to avoid. Which was so much cooler than sticking to the known routes. He just wished he could get Nashira to appreciate that. He'd switch places with her in a second—if he knew the first thing about piloting spaceships.

"I keep telling you, there's nothing glamorous about it," Nashira insisted. He hadn't said anything; she must've seen the look in his eyes as he watched her working the controls. "I just punch in the numbers they assign me and hope they don't come out in the middle of a star. I dive in, I climb out, I dive in again. I'm a bloody elevator operator."

"Yeah, but what an elevator!" She glared, and David figured he should've refined that metaphor a little more.

The voice of Nashira's supervisor came over the radio. *"Please try to stick to the assigned vectors today, Scout Wing,"* Vekredi said. *"I've received more complaints about your... improvisations. Any more and there will be penalties."*

"Shouldn't you be on maternity leave, Kred?" Nashira asked. "Your office is no place for nursing babies."

Indeed, David could hear peeping and suckling sounds over the speaker, followed by an offended snuffling from Vekredi. *"Just... follow the assigned schedule, Scout Wing! That is an order! Out."*

"How rude," Rynyan said. "One should always be courteous to one's inferiors."

Nashira threw him a glare, then smirked. "That explains it, then. Nobody's got more inferiority than Kred."

"So you want to ditch the plan anyway?" David ventured.

Nashira grinned at him, a refreshing change from her usual scowls. "Just to screw with him?" She thought about it. "Nahh. Not worth the penalties. Almost, though." She punched in the first vector, and the launch rail obligingly maneuvered the *Entropy* into position. In the viewing wall, the ships and equipment within the Shell wheeled dizzyingly, but the Hub itself, that strange, faintly glowing pucker of spacetime that David's eyes refused to focus on no matter how hard he tried, remained a fixed, unchanging point, the fulcrum around which galaxies revolved in more ways than one.

"Get your gizmos ready, we go in sixty," Nashira said. She glanced over as David activated the gravity sensor. "I thought you'd given up on that."

"I changed my mind. I was thinking about the Hub last night—how it's the center of mass of the Milky Way, its satellite galaxies, and its dark-matter halo?"

Nashira sighed. "Just say 'greater galaxy' like everyone else."

"Well, I thought about how an object acts like all its matter is concentrated at the center of mass. And the Hub acts like every point in the... the greater galaxy is concentrated in it. I think there's got to be a link there. Something to do with mass."

"Congratulations," Nashira said. "You've just discovered the first, most obvious theory that every civilization in history has come up with about the Hub. Only took you six weeks."

"Well, maybe they just gave up on it too easily."

"Or it's a dead end. Everyone agrees it's part of why the Hub exists, but it doesn't explain the link between vectors and destinations. If it's all clumped together, it should be random, not consistent for the same vector." She stared at him. "How can you be determined to learn the Hub's secrets and not know something this basic?"

"I didn't want to be trapped by past assumptions."

She rolled her eyes. "Oh, brilliant. This way you just repeat everyone else's failures. That's *much* better."

"Or try something they never thought of."

"I'll give you that. No genius in history has *ever* thought like you. Fifteen seconds."

David stared into the Hub, in awe of its cosmic centrality. Despite his outward confidence, Nashira's words were sobering. How could he believe that a college dropout from the backwater of the galaxy could succeed where so many advanced civilizations had failed?

Because there are no backwaters, he reminded himself. *Every point in nine galaxies is in there—all of them one, all of them equal. The Hub is inside me. I'm inside it. So I'm as worthy as anybody to figure it out.*

"Here we go," Nashira said. "Last chance to make your peace with the universe."

David smiled at her. "I'm good." She blinked, genuinely surprised.

Then Rynyan ruined the mood. "No problem. The universe and I are mutual fans."

Nashira sighed as the ship thrust forward into the center of all things...

And the alarms sounded. "Christ, we're in a gravity well!"

"Of what?" David cried.

"Won't matter unless we make orbital vee," she said, regaining the calm of a seasoned pilot. The fusion engines fired, pressing them back in their seats. Whatever they were trying to orbit was behind them, out of sight, and Nashira was too busy to work the aft sensors. David took it upon himself to switch the view.

"Uhh... Nashira?"

"In a mo."

"But—Okay, whenever you're ready."

"All right," Nashira said after a moment, looking up toward the display wall. "The ship can take it fro—*Holy Christ on a cassowary!*"

The planet below them was beautiful. Its sunlit half was shining blue oceans and vivid turquoise forests. Its nighttime half was festooned with city lights. The display wall called out thousands of satellites and stations in orbit. An inhabited, spacefaring civilization—the find of a lifetime for any Hub scout. "Nashira!" David cried. "This is—"

"Don't," Nashira said. "This can't be what it seems."

"But look, it's right there!"

"No, you don't get it. A Hub scout's lucky to make one major find in a lifetime. Two in as many months? No sodding way can that happen!"

"It's random. It's as likely as anything else." He smiled. "Maybe Rynyan and I are good luck charms."

"Rynyan." She whirled on the Sosyryn. "Don't you dare leave this cockpit! I will break your fucking legs before I let you steal another claim!"

But Rynyan was staring at the planet on the display wall. "Much as I love it when you get physical with me, my dear, I think the Ziovris would be rather annoyed if I tried to stake a claim."

"What have the Ziovris got to do with this?" Nashira asked. David recognized the name from news reports, a fairly prominent species in the Hub Network, but couldn't recall the specifics.

"Oh, you know how they are about their property. It totally

ruined my charity expedition here a few decades back. They nationalized all my donations! The Migration Bureau said they'd decide when and how to distribute them. So come tallying season I could only report one recipient from the whole expedition! It was a huge embarrassment. I was the laughing stock of all Rysos." He smiled. "Luckily Vnebnil was struck by that asteroid the following year. A prime donating opportunity there, and I was quick to get in on the ground floor."

Nashira glared at him. "I'm happy for you that all those people *died* so you could improve your social standing, but can we stay on topic? Where are we?"

"Why, the Ziovris homeworld, of course."

Nashira stared at the world on the viewer. Then she dove for the controls and spent several minutes verifying Rynyan's claim. "No, this... this can't be. I mean... no way could I make a find this great!" She was starting to grin despite herself.

But David was confused. "How can it be a great find if it's already in the Hub Network?"

"Damn, you really are from the middle of nowhere. And so's the Ziovris Hubpoint. It's thousands of AUs out in their cometary cloud. Months from here."

"Terribly inconvenient," Rynyan added. "Cold sleep simply ruins the sheen of my mane. That's the other reason I wouldn't want to claim this place. Oh, and the service? Simply terrible. I mean, sure, building a megastructure out at the Hubpoint and mobilizing the whole population to move there can be distracting, but it's simply no excuse for poor hospitality."

Nashira rolled her eyes. "Mr. Sensitive here's right about one thing. That remote Hubpoint's been rough on the Ziovris. Uprooting their whole civilization, sinking all their resources into the move... the strict rules they have to follow to keep that huge migration running smoothly... it's no way to live." She beamed. "Can you imagine what it'll mean to these people to gain a second Hubpoint practically right on their orbit?"

"Yeah," David breathed. A Hubpoint was a species' one and only link to the wealth and wonders of the galaxy. Hub contact had transformed Earth, bringing resources and technologies that offered greater prosperity than humanity had ever known—though far too gradually, at least until humanity could prove it had something to offer in return and become a genuine trading partner rather than a charity case. He recalled the long, expensive commute to Sol's Hubpoint just outside Saturn's orbit, and could understand why the Ziovris would be willing to relocate to their far more remote Hubpoint, as numerous other civilizations had in the past. But what might they give to be spared the trouble? "Nashira, this is great! You'll be rich! No, better, you'll be a hero!" Brightening, he reached out and grabbed her hand. "A human being finding something this important—Nashira, you've put us on the map!"

She blushed. "Well... you'll get your share of the fame too."

"I don't want fame for me. Just for humanity."

"Typical." She chuckled, and she didn't seem to be in any hurry to pull her hand away.

Then the alarms sounded again. Nashira spun to the controls. "Incoming ship! It's a military cruiser! They've got a laser lock on us, warning strength!"

"Quick, get us out of here!" Rynyan cried. "Especially me!"

"I can't! We've waited too long, the return beam's shut off! And there's no time to signal for a new one!" With the Hubpoint closed, they couldn't go anywhere except on the *Entropy*'s fusion drive, which was far less powerful than the warship's engines. "Bollocks!" Nashira cursed. "I knew this was too good to be true!"

A hail came in. Nashira accepted it promptly, not wishing to cause trouble. The being that appeared on the viewer had an upright body plan similar to a human's or Sosyryn's, but David could see other crew-beings in the background with four legs apiece, a forward-facing pair stacked atop a shorter rear-facing pair. Their skin was vivid blue and they bore elongated heads which resembled claw hammers from the side. *"This is Commander Relniv of the regulatory enforcement vessel* Mzinlix," intoned the officer in the foreground. *"Your presence in Ziovris orbital space is irregular, undocumented, and unauthorized. Identify yourselves and justify your departure from procedure."*

"This is Nashira Wing of the Hubdiver *Starship Entropy*.

I'm a Hub scout, Commander."

"No, you're not. No arrivals from the Hubpoint are scheduled. And your craft is not equipped for a journey of that duration."

"We didn't come from *that* Hubpoint, Commander." Nashira trembled with barely restrained excitement. "You're recording this, right? Well, I hereby inform you that I, Nashira Wing, Hub scout Blue 662 Red 769—"

"Of Earth," David interposed.

"—have just discovered a new Hubpoint in proximity to Ziovris's orbit."

Relniv stared. *"What? No. You've discovered no such thing. I say again, justify your departure from procedure or—"*

"No, ma'am, I swear." How Nashira could tell Relniv was female was beyond David. "The Hubpoint's closed now, but if you'll just let me send a quantelope signal back to the Hub, they'll reopen the vector and you can see the return beam for yourself."

"No unauthorized communications will be permitted. I have the authorization to fire upon you should you attempt it!"

"Um, excuse me," David put in. "Hi. David LaMacchia, also of Earth. Don't you see what this means, uh, ma'am? You have a Hubpoint right next to your planet now!"

"No," Relniv interjected. *"Just stop it. Cease these absurd claims at once."*

"I don't get it," David said. "I thought you'd be happy."

Rynyan stepped forward. "Here, I know how to handle this." He faced the Ziovris commander and gave her the Sosyryn equivalent of a smarmy grin. "Hello. I am Rynyan Zynara ad Surynyyyyyy'a, and I just want to say that whatever dole your government allots to you, it isn't nearly enough and I'd be happy to supplement it in exchange for your not shooting us. And may I also say you look very sexually desirable in that nice crisp uniform?"

"Rynyan!" Nashira pulled him away from the viewer and got in front of him. "Just ignore him, he's not with us, really. Look, no tricks, no bribes, just let me send one little 'lope message, please."

"*The policy on intruders in Ziovris airspace is very clear—no communication allowed.*"

"Why? Who could we contact that would hurt you? If there weren't a known Hubpoint nearby, then—"

"*Wait.*" Relniv took on the distant look of someone listening to a comm implant. "*I've received orders to secure your vessel and escort you to the surface. Do not attempt to disobey our instructions or the penalties will be severe.*"

"Okay, okay. We don't want any—"

"*And you will discuss this with no one.*" Relniv paused, listening to her comm again. "*What? Me? Sorry, I thought you meant... no, of course I won't discuss... but why...*" She straightened. "*Understood. Out.*" She sighed, looking thoughtful, maybe confused. It was hard to read a new species' expressions, but caution and hesitation could be recognized in most species' body language. Another common manifestation was a startled jump, which Relniv performed when she noticed that Nashira and the others were still watching her. "*You didn't hear that!*" she barked, and cut off the transmission.

3

Nashira was expecting a prison cell. So when Commander Relniv and her soldiers deposited them in a luxury hotel suite larger than Hubstation 3742's entire scout staging area, lavishly appointed with all the comforts she could imagine, it put her far more on edge.

"I couldn't agree with you more," Rynyan said once their escort had left them alone. "They expect me to stay here? I have toolsheds larger than this."

"Maybe they finally figured out this is good news and they're thanking us," David said.

Sometimes Nashira almost envied the kid for his simple idealism. Unfortunately, in practice it meant he'd probably get himself or others killed if she didn't babysit him constantly. "The way they made sure we couldn't contact anybody? More like they're fattening us up for the kill."

"Maybe they want it to be a surprise?"

Nashira just rolled her eyes.

"He has a point," Rynyan said. "News like this should be announced with proper pomp and ceremony. Music, parades, fireworks, gourmet feasts… local females hurling themselves at the feet of the heroic discoverers… ahhh. You know, the one good thing about my last visit was that those four legs allow for some very interesting positions."

"That much could be arranged," came a new voice. Nashira whirled. A fat, well-dressed Ziovris male stood in the doorway, flanked by Relniv and her guards. He had the look of a being who was well-fed, lazy, prone to overindulgences of all kinds, and dependent on advanced medicine to ease the ravages of that lifestyle. "Stay outside," he told Relniv.

"But, sir—"

He whirled on her, surprisingly fast for one of his bulk. "Did you say 'but'?"

Relniv lowered her elongated head. "No, sir."

"Of course you didn't." The fat male stepped inside, the door closing behind him. "Greetings. I am Cerou Gamrios, and on behalf of the Ziov Union I formally apologize for your cold welcome to Renziov. We would be happy to compensate you for your inconvenience. However, the... proper avenue for such compensation is not as, ah, public as you suggest."

"What the hell?" Nashira asked. "We just found a Hubpoint, mister. One practically right next to your planet."

"No, Scout Wing, you did not."

"Yes, we did! Don't you understand what this discovery means for your people?"

"I understand better than you, Scout Wing. And I assure you, you have not discovered a Hubpoint."

"Look, stop it, Ballpeenhead! I'm sick of the bureaucratic doublespeak!"

He went on as if she hadn't spoken. "And rest assured you will be richly rewarded for that non-discovery."

She blinked. "I'm listening."

"Nashira!" David cried.

"Why would you reward us for *not* helping your people?" Rynyan asked. "And more importantly, why didn't you compensate me the *last* time you stole credit for my aid?!"

"But you *would* be helping our people," Gamrios said. "You saw how distraught Commander Relniv was at the very suggestion of a new Hubpoint. Can you imagine that multiplied across our entire population?"

"But with a more convenient Hubpoint," Rynyan said, "you'd have no more of those nasty long commutes, those pathetic cubbyholes you call homes..."

"And you wouldn't need to waste all those resources on the move," David put in before Rynyan could make things any worse.

"Waste?" Gamrios asked. "The Union has spent a

generation organizing the most efficient, streamlined relocation of a planetary population in the history of the Network. Every move has been precisely calculated to optimize resources and energy. An entire planetary economy, infrastructure, and social order all completely devoted to a single massive undertaking, all executed with a discipline and commitment that makes the Ziovris the envy of the Network! Our people have dedicated their lives, not to mention their resources, to that undertaking: to systematically pack away an entire planet's wealth, technology, architecture, art, historical documents, flora, fauna, even the occasional natural wonder, and smoothly, economically relocate it all to our new world.

"If that great flow were interrupted, if we tried to halt or reverse its momentum, the waste would be unconscionable! Not only the waste of energy, the waste of time, the waste of resources—but the waste of our people's pride and dedication! Imagine the despair that would bring! To leave the great work unfinished—just because we don't *need* to do it? Unconscionable!"

"So you just keep on living in a police state for no reason?" David asked.

"Our discipline and self-sacrifice are reason in themselves. They give every one of us a purpose, a role to play in the great work. If a closer Hubpoint were found, then all of that meaning and structure, that sense of higher purpose, would be torn away, and what would be left to believe in?"

"How about the truth?" David said.

"Now, David," Nashira said. "The way I see it, everyone's entitled to their own belief systems."

"Nashira, they're trying to bribe us into lying!"

"There's no lie, and no bribe," Gamrios said cheerfully. "You did *not* discover that Hubpoint, and you will do our people a great service by not claiming its discovery." He went on before David could formulate a protest. "Just as I did them a service when *I* did not claim its discovery."

Nashira stared. "What?"

The fat Ziovris sighed. "As a youth, I chafed against the disciplines of our society and left home for the Hub in search of a new life. But thanks to my limited means, there was no place for me there save the role of Hub scout. Maybe it was before your time, or maybe our paths simply never crossed; yours is such a minor species, no offense." David fumed, but Nashira ignored it. "And one day, I took a dive through the Hub and found myself... home. Oh, Renziov was at a different point in its orbit, so I didn't arrive right above it as you did, but I knew my own sun, my own starscape."

"Wait." Nashira frowned. "They wouldn't send me on a known vector."

"Oh, they didn't." Gamrios trundled toward the window, gazing out at the gorgeous, sunlit oceanscape beyond. "I was filled with excitement at first. A convenient Hubpoint for Renziov! It would change everything. It would make me rich enough to get out of the life, famous enough to write my own ticket back home. I went back to the quantelope tank to report... and on the way, it hit me."

"What did?"

"Why, the sheer unlikelihood that I would emerge next to my own homeworld. That of all the scouts in the Hub, it was a Ziovris who found the Hubpoint near Renziov. That couldn't be random chance. That was *order*. Of all the scouts who could have discovered such a Hubpoint, the universe chose the one scout who would understand the importance of keeping it *un*discovered. I couldn't deny the synchronicity of that. I, Cerou Gamrios, had my own special role to play within the Great Migration. Even in my attempt at defiance, I had served the cause without knowing it.

"And once I recognized that, I understood how wrong it would be to disrupt that order. I realized how much our society depended on this grand, organized project in which every citizen, myself included, had a part to play. What is the Hub compared to that? The Network is too big, too expansive, too chaotic. The individual is lost in the shuffle. But here, everything fits together, everything makes sense, and everyone is needed in the great work. I couldn't take that away from my people by reporting what I'd found."

"Didn't you think your people deserved a say in that?" David pressed.

"Oh, they did. The Hubpoint beam on my arrival was detected by a nearby mining vessel and a regulatory enforcer. Independently, they both hailed me and begged me to tell them they hadn't seen what they thought they'd seen—that the commitment and sacrifices we've made still had meaning. I was happy to confirm that it was merely a glitch in my comm laser."

Gamrios straightened, insofar as his bulbous frame allowed. "Of course, this left me with a dilemma, for I could never return to the Hub. But as you can see," he went on, gesturing at the suite around them, "patriotism can have very tangible rewards. Those who became aware of my service to the Great Migration were happy to compensate me for my loss of employment. I was given a new identity and a, ah, position commensurate with the value of my service. I finally advanced," he said proudly, "but *within* the system, not despite it. Though I still have the Hub to thank."

"Oh my God," Nashira said. "Kred! That *diu puk gai!* He knew! He gave me a dead vector! He bloody tried to kill us!" She'd known a second discovery of this magnitude was too good to be true. It figured that it wasn't her discovery after all.

"Yes, I was surprised to see another scout so soon," Gamrios said. "That is my position in the system: to help ensure the continued non-discovery of the Hubpoint. It's an easy job, true, given the, ah, years between attempts, but you can't deny it's an essential one. The second scout came through at roughly the expected time, so my department was able to intercept him before he could alert the Hub. Yes, we weren't just sitting around earning a lavish state subsidy for nothing, we were *ready*." He fidgeted. "True, we, ah, weren't expecting the third for much longer, so no one can blame us for being a little slow on the response this time around. It's, ah, quite fortunate that you happened to materialize in our orbital space so you could be intercepted promptly."

"Fortunate for you, you mean," Nashira said.

"And for you as well, if you have the sense to follow my lead." He gestured out the window at the vista beyond—an expanse of rolling hills covered in forests of purple-fronded trees, bisected by a mighty river that issued from the base of a great, distant waterfall, its mists shimmering with red-skewed rainbows in the light of the K-type sun. "Look at it. All that vast, open beauty. Eventually there will be no one left on Renziov except for a very few who choose to remain isolated from the galaxy. And those few will have the resources of a whole world to divide among them. They will all be incredibly wealthy."

"So we stay here where nobody will ever find us, and live in luxury for the rest of our lives?"

"Exactly. Your predecessor scout was offered the same arrangement and wisely accepted. We've had no complaints."

Gamrios moved closer to her. "And why wouldn't he? You know what the life of a scout is like as well as I do. The constant danger... the endless tedium... the meager rewards. Who wouldn't give up that life in a heartbeat if offered something better? What loyalty do you owe to someone who tried sending you to your death?"

As her fellow scout held her eyes, Nashira found she couldn't dismiss his words. Find a paradise planet and retire there without ever telling the boss? It was every Hub scout's secret fantasy.

She smiled at Gamrios. "Why don't you let me think about it for a while?" she said. Just because it was her fantasy, that didn't mean she couldn't milk it for all the Ziovris were worth.

4

The suite's facilities were indeed luxurious. Rynyan wasted no time sampling the food printer and the bar, while Nashira availed herself of a bathtub big enough to qualify as an Olympic pool. David left them to it. He needed to think for a while.

When Nashira came out of the bathroom wrapped in a towel—a rather small one, since most Ziovris had slimmer frames than humans—she was indignant to find David leaning against the wall right outside the bathroom door. "What are you doing here?" she exclaimed, tightening her grip on the towel.

"Keeping watch," he said. "In case Rynyan tried to peek at you or something."

"Oh." Her gaze softened. "That's... really sweet." She seemed to mean it, but she also seemed vaguely disappointed for some reason David couldn't figure. Maybe she was just disappointed not to have something to yell about. She couldn't let herself be happy or optimistic about anything. David liked to think he'd taught her a thing or two about hope over the past month, though. She smiled more these days than when they'd first met.

But David wasn't in the mood to smile. For once, he felt he had to be the skeptical one. As she headed for her room, he stepped in her path. "Nashira, we have to talk."

She held his gaze. "I'm listening."

She was breathing heavily, her stare intense. David realized he was standing awfully close, probably making her nervous. He stepped back, looking away. "I... I mean after you get dressed."

"Oh. Of course." There was that weird sense of disappointment again. It was like she'd have been happier if he'd stayed in her personal space so she could be mad at him. She swept past him and into her room. She let the scant towel fall a little too soon, and he quickly looked away. He'd be a poor friend and partner if he let himself notice her in that way. And she'd probably kill him if she knew he'd seen her butt. He tried not to think about it.

But boy, she sure was fit.

Luckily, he had his concerns to keep him distracted. "Are you really going to go along with this?" he asked Nashira once she emerged, attired in a fetching blue dress that the suite's fabricator must have made for her.

"Look around, kid," she said with a laugh. "This is the good life! Everything I could ever want at my fingertips, a whole planet to wander around in without a lot of people to bother me, and best of all, no more daily risk of instant death or terminal boredom. No more Kred looking down his little rat nose at me."

"But what about our quest? What about humanity?"

She fell back onto an enormous couch. "*Your* quest was a fantasy. Humanity's got nothing new to offer the Network, and we're lucky to get the charity we do. Things are decent now for folks back home; why make waves?"

"Because decent isn't good enough. Because there's a whole galaxy of wonders we deserve to be a part of."

"Even so, you and I weren't going to change things. You don't know what you're doing, and I don't ruddy care."

David sighed. "Do you care about the Ziovris? Is it really okay with you to get this kind of luxury in exchange for helping a government keep lying to its people?"

"That's what governments do. They're all scams to keep people in line."

"No, they aren't. Look at the Sosyryn. Everyone's free and equal there."

"That just means everyone's in on the scam. They scam themselves into thinking their condescending charity gives meaning to their empty lives, and they scam rubes like you into thinking it makes them nobler than the rest of us." She shook her head. "Do-gooders are just as self-serving as everyone else. They just get rewarded in ego points." She leaned back and stroked the couch's velvety contours. "Me, I'd rather get more tangible rewards."

"Hmph," said Rynyan, who'd wandered over after hearing his people mentioned. "You call this a reward? The minibar only serves eighty kinds of liquor. And I checked—they only have ten masseuses on call and only six will take their clothes off!"

"Oh, learn to rough it."

"I 'rough it' quite enough slumming in your squalid little Hubstation. I want to go home!"

"And how are you going to arrange that, hmm?"

"Didn't you see the way that female guard was looking at me?" Rynyan preened his feathery mane. "Leave it to me, I'll persuade her to let us out of here."

Nashira stood to face him, having some difficulty getting off the pillowy couch. "Try it and you'll get us all in trouble!"

"Exactly," David said. "We have to be united in this. We need you with us, Nashira. Please."

"David, it's okay. Just immerse yourself in the luxury and let it wash those pesky ideals away. You'll be happier."

"Would *you* really be happy here? What about... companionship? Human... companionship?"

She looked at him through lowered lashes, a rakish tilt to one brow. "That could be arranged."

"How? By having the suite fabricate a man for you? Get real, Nashira!"

"Oh, the hell with you!" she cried, turning to stride away. "Go on, try to escape, get your arse thrown in prison for all I care."

"We're already in prison." That froze her in her tracks. David went to her, turning her around and gripping her bare shoulders. "Look, you're the one always complaining about a Hub scout's life. How oppressed and hopeless you are. This whole world's like that. Every Ziovris is living the life you want to get away from. Worse—a life that people would take up Hub scouting to *escape*."

"It's what they've chosen. It matters to them."

"It's what they've learned to settle for," David countered. "Because they've lost hope that things can change. Because they're afraid to let themselves believe there can be a better life."

He clasped her hands, looking deep into her eyes. "Do you really want to be like them, Nashira? At least in the Hub, you have a chance. You have something to strive for. To hope for. Are you really ready to give that up?"

After a moment, she turned away, storming over to the picture window to gaze out at the blazing, gorgeous sunset. "You are so ... damn ... selfless. Didn't say a word about what you wanted, didn't try to get me to do it for you." She whirled. "It's not fair, you know. Makes me feel inadequate for being selfish."

"You're not selfish, Nashira. You just want a better life. We all do. Including the Ziovris."

She winced and clenched her fists, letting out a shriek. "Okay, then. Let's do this before I bloody change my mind. Or just strangle you."

"Great!" David cried. "On to freedom!"

She rolled her eyes. "But I'm keeping the damn dress."

Rynyan's plan to seduce the guard proved disturbingly successful. Nashira couldn't understand why a self-respecting female of any species would fall for his bald advances. But it didn't take Rynyan long at all to talk the guard into trying out the bathtub with him while allowing the humans to slip away. Maybe the Ziovris were just too accustomed to being submissive, and the guard had responded to the Sosyryn's air of superiority and entitlement. Not that Rynyan would see it that way; to him, he was doing the guard a favor. *Better her than me*, Nashira thought. And then she tried very hard not to think about it anymore.

Which just led her to think about her own sexual prospects. *"That could be arranged?" What was I thinking? A lifetime here with David as my only possible lover?* Okay, he was reasonably cute in a lost-puppy kind of way... and sweet... and generous... and kind... and sometimes when he gazed into her eyes and made those passionate, idealistic speeches, it stirred something inside her that she thought she'd lost a long time ago... but no. He was pure man-child. Completely immature, and not even in the fun way. Her flirtations had gone right over his head;

even flashing her bum hadn't gotten a rise. She must've been desperate even to try it—so blinded by the wealth and luxury Gamrios offered that she forgot how much she'd miss the company of real men. The hell with the plight of the Ziovris people—she was escaping in the name of getting well and properly laid ever again.

Not to mention the reward for finding the new Hubpoint. It might not be wealth as endless as what Gamrios had been peddling, but she could still come out of this a rich woman.

And, okay, helping the Ziovris throw off the yoke of oppression would be nice too. It wasn't like she had anything against them.

Though when they reached the door to the quantelope shack and Commander Relniv emerged with her firearm pointed right at Nashira's chest, she began to rethink that opinion.

"Why are you here?" Relniv asked.

"Us? Oh, nothing, we were just... looking for the gym." Nashira shut herself up before she said anything stupider.

So naturally David did it for her. "We're trying to escape, Commander. Holding us here is wrong."

"No," Relniv said. "I mean, why are you *here*?" She gestured around at the luxurious facility. "Why would they take you to this place?" Nashira belatedly recognized the dismay and confusion in the commander's alien features. "If you were lying about a new Hubpoint, *why would they reward you?*"

"Because we're not lying," David said. "They are. And they don't want us to tell anyone."

"No." The crests at the rear of her head quivered in negation. "Tell me it's not true. Tell me there's no Hubpoint. Tell me there's some other reason you're here. It has to be a lie!"

David frowned. "Why?"

Relniv stared at him. "The system exists for a purpose. I have my own role to play, my duties to fulfill, and there's a reason for it all. There has to be. If there isn't... if there's a closer Hubpoint and we don't have to migrate after all... then all the sacrifices I've made..." She looked away. "All the sacrifices I've... enforced... will have been for nothing. For a lie. My whole life... it will have been meaningless."

David stepped closer and did that sincere thing with his face. "It doesn't have to be," he told Relniv. "You can give your life a new meaning. A better meaning. Help us help your people."

Relniv's weapon hand wavered and lowered. Nashira's first impulse was to knock it out of her hand, punch her lights out, and step over her trembling body to get to the quantelopes. Somehow, though, she found herself waiting, giving David's way a chance to work.

"But what would happen?" Relniv asked. "It would be chaos. We've already shipped out so many of us, so much of what we have. If that movement stopped… it would be so hard to reverse it, to get things back."

"That's what Mr. Gamrios said," David replied. "But it seems to me, there's a Hubpoint here and there's a Hubpoint out there." He shrugged. "Maybe you're far apart the normal way, but you're right next door the Hub way. So you don't have to stop or reverse anything. Just keep going forward, then bring it right back around through the back door.

"Or some of you could stay out there and others could stay here. You'd be only moments apart through the Hub. Okay, hours. Maybe days, if it's really busy. But that's better than months. There'd be no need to fight over where to live. You'd still be one society."

Relniv still hesitated. "But the great machine… it has so much inertia. There are so many who won't want things to change … or who won't know how. They'll resist—by force if necessary."

"Not to worry!" It was Rynyan, who'd arrived behind them, smelling of what Nashira hoped was just his species' version of sweat. "The Sosyryn would be glad to exert our diplomatic clout toward ensuring a smooth transition. If all your bureaucrats are as fond of bribery as Mister Gamrios, it should be easy enough. And I personally will be happy to see to the needs of any Ziovris who fall victim to whatever social upheavals may result in the meantime." His mane trembled with his excitement. "That will more than make up for my last visit here," he told Nashira. "I knew the universe would make amends for that little embarrassment in time."

Relniv had mercifully ignored that last part, squeezing her eyes shut as she wrestled with her conscience. Finally, she met David's eyes. "I don't know if I can do this. All my life, I've known my purpose, had my place prepared for me. If I do this, I have no idea what will lie ahead."

David smiled. "I know that feeling. I've felt it every day since I left home for the Hub."

"And... how do you endure it?"

"Endure it? I love it! Where's the fun in a story where you always know what happens next?"

Relniv looked confused, but there was something contagious about David's enthusiasm. "This will violate so many regulations... they'll send me to an asteroid mine for the rest of my life."

"You can come with us. There's a whole universe out there."

She looked tempted, but finally said, "No. This is my home. I'll take my chances. And maybe... maybe those regulations won't apply anymore." She looked shocked at even being able to formulate the concept—but excited that she had.

David clasped her hand and they went into the quantelope shack together. Nashira couldn't resist glancing back at Rynyan, though. "The way you talked about it, I thought you and that lady guard would be at it a lot longer."

Rynyan puffed out his chest and his mane. "My dear, when you're as skilled in the arts of sex as I am, you don't need long at all."

5

Soon after Nashira notified the Hub of her discovery—and her distress—a flotilla of ships belonging to the Mkubnir, one of the species that cooperated in overseeing Hub Network security, emerged through the new Hubpoint, revealing its existence for all to see. The escapees were soon intercepted by Gamrios' forces, but the bloated bureaucrat had already been warned by the Mkubnir that no harm must come to the Hub scout or her passengers. Nashira enjoyed watching him squirm as he offered to escort them back to the *Starship Entropy*.

The only thing better was the look on Mokak Vekredi's face when she stormed into his office back at the Hubstation. The hermaphrodite was nursing "his" babies when she charged in, and he squawked and ducked behind the desk—though whether it was to hide the evidence of Zeghryk prolificacy or merely to hide from her wrath was unclear. "Scout Wing! You should not be in here without invitation!"

"Stow it, Kred. Be glad your babies are here, since they're the only thing keeping me from ripping your little buckteeth out. I took a look at the dive logs when I got back, did some digging to find out how a dormant vector got on my dive schedule, and guess whose authorization code I found on the system access."

Kred trembled in fear, peeping almost as pathetically as the babies. "I was only following orders, Scout Wing!"

She waved it aside. "Of course you were. That's all you know how to do." She strode forward to stand before his desk, gazing intimidatingly down at his hunkered form. "It doesn't bother me so much that you tried to kill me—again. That's more or less in your job description. But going after civilians is another matter.

"So you tell your Dosper bosses: I'm willing to keep quiet about their attempt on our lives. Everybody's so thrilled about the new Ziovris Hubpoint—no sense ruining that with a scandal. But only if they leave David and me alone." She paused. "And Rynyan, I guess. Anything happens to us, those access records gets released. Got it?"

"I-I will convey that information."

"Good." She flopped back into a chair and put her feet up on his desk. "Now, there's the little matter of my finder's fee to talk about." It sent an almost sexual thrill through Nashira to say it. The reporters were already calling this the find of the century, or whatever units they used. Between that and her blackmail power, she could make enough from this to leave the Hub scout life behind forever and never have to put up with David LaMacchia and Rynyan again.

But David will be lost without you, she told herself.

Shut up. I'll hire him a babysitter.

But Kred was straightening up and gaining more confidence than he should have at this point in the conversation. In fact, he even seemed to be doing the Zeghryk equivalent of smiling. "What... fee... would that be, Ms. Wing?"

"No games, Kred!"

"Ah, for the record, Ms. Wing."

She leaned forward and spoke slowly and loudly. "My bonus for discovering the new Ziovris Hubpoint."

Kred continued to smile. "As I understand it, that Hubpoint was actually discovered by a Ziovris scout some seventeen years ago."

"Who forfeited his rights by failing to report it. I reported it, so I get the reward!"

"Ah, I see. Here is the crux of your misunderstanding: To receive a Hubpoint discovery bonus from the Hub administration, one must be acting in the capacity of a Hub scout."

Nashira stared in disbelief. "Hello? Who've you been calling 'Scout Wing' all this time?"

"A temporary error, *Ms.* Wing, arising from my distress. You see, when you failed to report after your initial dive yesterday,

I naturally followed proper procedure and had you declared dead."

She gaped. "What? I'm *dead?*"

"At the moment, yes." He tilted his head. "Technically, I shouldn't even be speaking to you. It could constitute either evidence of mental illness or an inappropriate on-duty religious observance."

"Kred!"

"And since you were therefore not a Hub employee—or even legally a person—at the time the new Ziovris Hubpoint was reported, it has been classed as a Ziovris discovery which went unreported due to negligence and fell into default. Thus, the Dosperhag have claimed it as a windfall. All profits from its discovery go to the Hub administration. Which, naturally, will set aside a generous reserve thereof for investment in the restoration of the Ziovris economy. After all, we are all neighbors in the Network."

Nashira shot to her feet. "So I get nothing? Not even credit for finding it?" To her surprise, she felt angrier on David's behalf than hers. Having humans make this discovery wouldn't have counted for as much as he thought—any moron in a Hubdiver could've done the same—but it would've been good publicity, at least.

"You get to live, Ms. Wing, and to be left alone by the Dosperhag. Count yourself fortunate."

"And what if I threaten to expose what I know if I don't get what's owed me?"

Kred leaned forward, carefully sheltering his nursing young in his arms. "Understand, Ms. Wing. The Dosperhag have the resources of the entire Hub Network at their disposal. Any evidence you have, they can counter or eradicate. I believe they can be persuaded to leave you and your... colleagues alone in exchange for avoiding a public scandal, but if you create such a scandal, they will punish you, and you will end up wishing you had not returned from that dive."

Nashira was sobered. They had her totally beaten, coming and going. She would kill David for convincing her to leave Renziov, if she didn't feel so bad for him right now. Though she was sure he'd get over it quickly and find hope in his next lunatic scheme. And Rynyan, as usual, had come out ahead on the whole deal. So as usual, Nashira Wing was the only one who got screwed—and not in the fun way.

Kred looked at her with feigned sympathy. "I understand this is difficult for you, Ms. Wing. If it would help, you could always apply for the Hub scout position left vacant by your tragic death...."

QUARTERLY DIGEST OF THE HUB SCOUTING GUILD (EXCERPT)

ND 23,409/7792-19.PUCE

...Congratulations to Scout Ognip Ourellzeb Ofierini Ob of Hubstation 803 for her discovery of a new technological civilization! This spacefaring species calls itself the Soijt, and remarkably, it has already made contact with another sapient race within normal-space travel range! Little is yet known about this second civilization, but as Hub contact experts refine their knowledge of Soijt language and culture, it is hoped that this impressively advanced new species will prove key to bringing not just one, but two new civilizations into the Network. Scout Ob's discovery has earned her a rare double bonus, enabling her both to pay off her debts *and* to purchase a private estate on the Inner World of the Ipqo Rosette. We wish Scout Ob the best in her new life. Remember—one day this may be you!

Congratulations also to Scout Mmorreff Ssukkll, who retired with honors this past quarter. Ssukkll is the first Hub scout in four years to survive to retirement age, a truly impressive feat—even granting that Ssukkll is a member of the Hhunnttikk (Hubstation 1968) with a life expectancy of 23 years. As we always say, it's not how long you live, but how much you achieve!

Fallout is still ongoing from the scandal surrounding the unreported second Ziovris Hubpoint, as revealed by an investigation conducted by noted philanthropist and sexual adventurer Rynyan Zynara ad Surynyyyyy'a. Two Hub scouts previously reported dead, Scout Cerou Gamrios (Hubstation 3634) and Scout Memnor of the Maximum Squealing (Hubstation

2320), are now in custody for conspiracy to defraud the Network. If they are convicted, their families will be required to refund their death benefits, although Mr. Zynara has promised to compensate said families for any losses. A third scout briefly reported dead in the incident, Scout Nashira Wing (Hubstation 3742), has also been investigated, with inconclusive results. Scout Wing listed no family or beneficiaries for her death benefits, instead bequeathing them to her fellow Hub scouts for the purposes of, as stipulated in her contract, "a night of drunken debauchery in [her] honor." Since the combined repair, medical, and legal fees resulting from this observance exceed the total of Scout Wing's benefits and savings, the balance will be deducted from her future salary. A preliminary draft of this document was released with Scout Wing's name in the memorial section (see screens 16-22 below); we regret the error.

All Hub scouts are reminded that the next round of quantelope maintenance seminars, "Quantelope Breeding and Entanglement Renewal," will commence at the onset of the next quarter. Remember, these refresher courses are mandatory! As recent events remind us, you must never take your quantelopes' safety for granted—they need you almost as much as you need them!

MAKE HUB, NOT WAR

1

The Soijt invasion of the Hub had been the most entertaining thing to happen to Rynyan in months. He was disappointed that it had ended so quickly.

After all, given that the Hub was the only known method of faster-than-light travel, it was excitingly rare for any new contactee to have a history of space warfare. But sometimes the Hub scouts stumbled across a world with nearby enemies—either in the same system or around an exceptionally close neighbor star—and the first thing they would do after Network contact was to try sending a war fleet through the Hub. That part had been a stimulating novelty for Rynyan, a charming departure from the usual routine of life at the Hubcomplex.

But what had followed had been eminently predictable. Like all such aspiring invaders, the Soijt had been fouled up in the machinery of the Shell surrounding the Hub, then smacked down easily by the mighty defense forces that cooperated in its protection. The excitement had quickly ended, and as was all too often the case in life, the boring part was now lasting far longer.

Case in point: Due to the current limitations on intracomplex flights due to the drifting debris from the invasion attempt, Rynyan had been forced to travel between rings via the hyperway like a mere charity case. He'd offered to shuttle Nashira Wing and David LaMacchia across to Hubstation 9 in his personal skiff; even if the good faith the Sosyryn had earned through their many past donations weren't sufficient to get a travel exemption, Rynyan was sure he could offer sufficient personal donations to bring it about. But David wouldn't hear of it; true to form, he was fascinated by the hyperway, which took advantage of the same quirk of Hub-adjacent spacetime that made his tesseract-shaped hotel suite possible. "Just imagine," the young human rhapsodized as they waited at the dingy platform. "Getting from ring to ring by a shortcut through the fourth dimension! Isn't it incredible?"

Rynyan laughed. "A shortcut? Goodness, no, it's actually a slightly longer trip. We are taking a detour through an extra dimension, after all."

"Yeah," Nashira confirmed. "Even here, space isn't *that* curved."

Once they boarded the car, even David had to confess that it was little different from the subways of Earth's major cities. What with the travel restrictions, the train was especially crowded, with hundreds of bodies from dozens of species pressed firmly together. Rynyan wasn't even able to bribe any wall-berth occupants into surrendering their places to him; not only were the berths prime real estate in these conditions, but there simply wasn't room to push through the crowd of straphangers to swap positions. So he had to dangle in free fall like the common folk around him, yanked around by the train's accelerations; the cars had their own nanofog, but the heavy flow of passengers boarding and debarking inevitably eroded the supply of nanites, so the inertial damping grew less effective after every stop. And Nashira insisted that David stay between the two of them, so Rynyan didn't even get the consolation of feeling Nashira's body press against his as the train accelerated. And David was too determined to be "just friends" with Nashira to let himself enjoy that experience. Which just confirmed what Rynyan had known from the start: the lad was categorically insane. But then, that was what made him such a worthwhile and entertaining charity case—most of the time.

"This isn't the way it's supposed to work," Rynyan complained to his favorite human playmates as they finally disembarked into the Sosyryn sector of Hubstation 9, located in one of the innermost, highest-class habitat rings that circled the Hub. "The way it's supposed to work," he said to Nashira, "is that you take us on random Hub dives in your ship, and you," he went on to David, "try to use your quaint Earth 'science' to crack the secret of predicting Hub vectors, while I wear down Nashira's denial of her passionate desire for me." Nashira scoffed quite loudly. Rynyan preened his slightly disheveled mane, confident from his extensive studies of human erotic literature (or "pr0n") that her resistance was merely a disguise for her true feelings. "And we even manage to have the occasional adventure along the way.

"But this is just tedious. Sitting around in your dreary Hubstation, doing nothing for days at a time... this is not a satisfying return on my investment!"

To be sure, boredom was a common complaint of the Sosyryn people. Commerce through the Hub had brought them endless riches, letting them shape their star system into a paradise free of want or peril. Which was certainly better than the squalid little lives of, say, humans, but it brought its own problems, chief among them the lack of sufficient stimulation to fill a Sosyryn's extremely long life. Which was why so many Sosyryn took vicarious enjoyment from watching—that is, helping to ease—the suffering and toil endured by the poorer races of the galaxy. Charity projects like underwriting David's research gave Rynyan's life its purpose, its meaning. They gave him something to *do*.

David gaped in wonder at the sights that unfolded before him as they exited the hyperway terminal into the Hubstation proper. "You brought us here. That counts for something."

The Sosyryn sector was a welcome sight for Rynyan after the squalor of the more remote Hubstation assigned to Earth. Although both catered to oxy-water bipeds from intermediate-gravity worlds, they had little else in common. HS9 catered to the most prosperous, powerful bipeds in the Hub Network, boasting state-of-the-art technology that made HS3742's facilities look like mud huts and stone axes. Instead of cramped, dingy corridors and chambers, it boasted vast, open expanses of planetformed landscape beneath a purple-blue sky. Through the translucent illumination provided by the roof kilometers above, one could see the habitat ring curving upward in both directions, its arms rising to embrace the innermost administrative ring, the free-orbiting defense satellites, and the gleaming sphere of the Shell. The Central Bulge was half-risen in the antispinward sky, filling one whole side of the sky with a solid wall of nacreous starlight. Even Nashira seemed grudgingly impressed at the sight.

Rynyan escorted the humans through a broad plaza lined with Rysosian *hkyryh* trees and explicitly carved Sosyryn fertility icons, which David examined with a tourist's fascination and Nashira sighed and rolled her eyes at. He would have been happy to regale Nashira at length on the rich erotic symbolism of the icons, but the hyperway trip had left him famished, so he continued to lead them toward his favorite Pajhduh restaurant—having already run a biochemical check to ensure that Pajhduh cuisine would be reasonably nonlethal to their species. "Don't misunderstand," he told them, resuming his lament. "I'm perfectly happy to throw my money away on a hopeless cause. That's the essence of charity, after all. But at least it should *look* like it's accomplishing something! Why can't the repair teams just hurry up and get it over with?"

"Still quite a mess to clean up inside the Shell," Nashira told him, looking radiant in the outdoor lighting as she brushed her long, silky black hair away from her piercing dark eyes. "You can't bribe them into repairing it faster. Nonessential travel like Hub scouting will just have to wait a while longer," she said with a grin, pleased for the respite from the tedious, dangerous work.

David was shaking his head, gazing up at the Shell and wearing that human expression Rynyan had learned to recognize as idealistic wonder—a look he'd never seen on Nashira's face. "That's one of the most amazing things about the Hub. Everyone who wants to travel beyond their own star system has to pass through here, so nobody can get away with an invasion. Nobody can build an empire or fight an interstellar war. Everyone works together protecting the Hub because they all need it. And so the greater galaxy has been at peace for over fifteen thousand years. It's a miracle."

"Yeah, sure," Nashira said, smirking. "And just think: if you figure out how the Hub works, people will be able to build new ones or invent faster-than-light drives, and then they'll be free to conquer and slaughter anyone they want! Won't that be *nifty?*"

David stared for a long moment. He looked shaken to the bone at having one of his core assumptions challenged. Oh, this was entertaining to watch!

"No, it's... I mean, they might not... you don't really think they'd..."

Nashira sighed and took pity on him. "Forget it, kid, I'm just messing with you. I'm sure your breakthrough will bring peace and love and kittens to everyone."

They soon reached the restaurant, whereupon the Pajhduh server showed them to Rynyan's permanently reserved table, managing to keep his overt scorn for the humans to a minimum out of deference to a loyal customer. "Now, as I was saying," Rynyan went on once they'd placed their orders, "if you can't make any Hub dives for now, I may need to find another cause that will let me donate more effectively." He increasingly worried about his standing as the next tallying season approached. His insatiably charitable cousin Hyryl had virtually bankrupted herself to endow the construction of radiation shields for a heavily settled binary system in danger from a nearby supernova. Of course, she'd quickly recovered thanks to Rysos's nigh-inexhaustible communal treasury and the charity of dozens of minor Sosyryn donors trying to boost their own tallies, but right now her prestige was through the roof and Rynyan couldn't bear to see her show him up for the twenty-ninth season running.

David looked worried, but Nashira simply grinned. "You hear that, LaMacchia? Your sugar daddy's cutting you off. You may actually have to get a job if you want to stay here."

"No, Rynyan, you can't!" David protested. "It'll just be a little while longer. And I can do my research without making dives. I can study my readings, consult local scientists—come on, you gotta help me out here!"

"Oh, stop whining," Nashira said. "I work for a living, why should you be any different?"

David fidgeted. "It's just... I've never really had much skill for, well, finding jobs. Or… keeping them."

"Figures."

"I just can't commit myself to a job that doesn't inspire me. I can't waste my life on something ordinary and meaningless. That's why I came out here in the first place."

Rynyan appreciated David's efforts to reaffirm his dependence, but he'd have to think about it later, for the food had arrived. It was a pleasure to have a decent meal after slumming in that low-class Hubstation for so long. Yet Rynyan had consumed everything on the Pajhduh restaurant's menu so many times that it was more an expected comfort than the exciting novelty it was for David and Nashira. At least, he was pretty sure they enjoyed it. Humans grimaced in orgasm, he knew, so their expressions and moans as they ate suggested they must be in ecstasy. He envied them.

But at least there were some engagingly exotic females to watch. (Males and other sexes too, he supposed, but he wasn't currently inclined their way. He underwent neurological and hormonal adjustment every few decades to reorient his sexual tastes for variety's sake, and he was now in the early years of an exclusively gynephilic phase—to Nashira's feigned disappointment and, he was sure, her eventual profound gratification.) Few new bipedal species had joined the Network in recent decades, but while Rynyan's tastes ran to novelty, there was still a wealth of variety even in a single species' females or approximate equivalents. Like that splendidly angular Heurhot at the bar. Her head-spines were long and multihued, her legs long and jointed like a Terran feline's, the three wide, wedge-shaped mammary glands stacked atop one another on her chest tapering nicely to the corners…

Wait. He recognized those corners. And more.

He turned away, hoping she hadn't seen him. "Nashira, switch seats with me."

She stared. "What, so you can get off on the warmth from my bum?"

"No! Though come to think of it—" He shook his feathery mane. "Never mind. I don't want that Heurhot to see me. No, don't look!"

But of course she was looking. "Mmm, she's a choice one. Old flame? Or a jealous spouse?"

"A former sexual associate, nothing more."

"What's her name?" David asked.

"Details." Rynyan waved off the question.

Nashira stared. "No wonder you don't want her to see you, *Rynyan*." She spoke his name rather loudly.

"It's not that," he said. "I simply had my fill of her and moved on. I seek *novel* experiences."

The human pilot studied him. "Wait. You mean if I actually gave in and let you root me, you'd lose interest and stop bothering me?"

"Well, after a few weeks." Rynyan preened. "The most intense and exciting few weeks of your—"

"Naah. So very much not worth it."

"Rynyan? Rynyan Zynara ad Surynyyyyyy'a? It is you!"

The voice was distinctly Heurhot in timbre, and the way she trilled his clan name was distinctly familiar. (So few non-Sosyryn caught on that the third *y* was silent.) He tried to hide his face and mutter something about mistaken identity, but Nashira beamed and said, "Well, hello there! Rynyan was just telling us about you! I'm Nashira and this is David. We're *so* pleased to meet another of Rynyan's friends! Won't you join us, er... ?"

"Aytriaew. Thank you, I'd be delighted." She gave Rynyan a firm hug, those wedges digging sharply (but, alas, familiarly) into his chest. "It's exquisite to see you again, Rynyan. How do your charities fare?"

As reluctant as he was to lead her on, he couldn't resist that question. "Oh, marvelously," he embellished. "In fact, my companions here are my current pet project." He went on to tell Aytriaew about Earth, playing up the primitiveness of its society, their habits of warfare and ecological destruction, and their lowly status in the Network to make them sound as desperately in need of his aid as possible. "As it happens, David here is on a quest of sorts to raise Earth's status by—you'll love this, I swear it's not a joke—"

But Aytriaew interrupted him, her head-spines straightening

in excitement. "Wait. Earth? Of course, Earth! Well, isn't this the most extraordinary happenstance? I represent a charitable group of my own, and we've been planning to provide aid to Earth ourselves! That's why I wanted to speak to you. You see, we need your help."

"Oh? Oh!" Rynyan was relieved. Here he thought she'd been plying him for more sex—a perfectly reasonable assumption, since he'd surely left her immensely satisfied—but instead she was seeking his charitable services. "Well, of course we Sosyryn exist to aid those in need. Please tell me what I can do for you."

"Wait a minute," Nashira interrupted, facing Aytriaew. "If you're doing charity on Earth, how come you didn't recognize our species?"

"Well, I wouldn't have expected to see your kind in a restaurant like this, dear. It was hard to recognize you without the squalor."

"Hey!" David protested.

"Oh, but you clean up very nicely, I'm sure."

Rynyan interposed. "Now, what about this aid you needed from me?"

Aytriaew's large, purple eyes turned to him again. "Well, we were all ready to begin shipping supplies to Urt—ahh, Earth—when that horrible Soijt invasion happened. And you know how it is when some new group of savages tries to start one of their silly wars. Everyone's so panicked about the threat of harm to the Hub, or of someone sneaking weapons through, that the administration has to institute the most stringent security precautions for however long it takes to reassure everyone. All those scans and searches." She bared her sharp teeth, her spines pointing back and darkening. "The sheer invasiveness of it, having my innards probed through the fourth dimension. I ask you, what happens if the pressure field breaks down and my organs leak out into hyperspace?"

"Well, it's the price we must pay for peace, my dear," Rynyan pointed out, though of course the "we" was a polite fiction. "And I don't see why it would prevent a relief shipment from going through."

"Some of our cargo consists of... sensitive experimental

medicines. These humits are a new species—"

"Humans," David corrected.

"Yes, and treating them requires creating new molecular compounds and nanosystems. If they're passed through a four-dimensional scanner and the containment fields aren't perfectly aligned, there could be unpredictable rotations in their molecular matrices. It could render them useless or toxic."

"Ahh," Rynyan said. "You need my help getting them through customs."

"Of course. Everyone knows the Sosyryn are above reproach. No one would think to suspect you of any nefarious dealings."

Nashira scoffed. "Seriously? I could tell you some of the shit he's pulled—"

"All in pursuit of the greater good," he reminded her.

"*Your* greater good."

"The Sosyryn's great generosity is universally respected," Aytriaew insisted. "Any customs official who might seek to question or impede you, Rynyan, could surely be... persuaded to grant you passage in exchange for a demonstration of that generosity."

"It's true. I have found bribery a very useful tool. And claimable as an additional donation."

"Then you'll do it?"

"Why, certainly!" Rynyan crowed. "I welcome the opportunity to visit Earth and show them my generosity at first hand." He turned to David and Nashira. "And you two simply must come with me. You can show me around!"

"Fantastic!" David said. "You'll love my mom, and my brother, and—"

"Yes, yes, whatever. Ahh, Nashira, I see you're grimacing in ecstasy at the thought!"

She stared. "What? No! I mean... No," she went on after a moment. "You go, have fun back in Hooterville. My life is here now."

"Come on, Nashira," David said. "You haven't seen Earth for, what, over nine years? It's getting better, you know. You might be surprised how much you miss it."

Her eyes flashed in that way Rynyan found so charming, but

she restrained herself and spoke more calmly. "Well… maybe. But what are the odds that Kred will authorize my leave?"

"It's not like he needs you for anything right now," David said. "I'm sure he'll understand."

She gave a weak grin. "Heh. We can only hope."

"Absolutely not!" said Mokak Vekredi, to Nashira's great relief. "Scout Wing has duties here."

Rynyan leaned across Vekredi's disproportionately massive desk, his leonine features taking on a look he believed to be endearing. "What duties, my friend? She's just sitting idle until normal Hub service resumes."

"Which could be at any time." A diminutive mole-like head, a smaller and far cuter version of Kred's own, poked over his shoulder—one of Kred's recent litter, already quadrupled in size in the two months since its birth, clinging to its hermaphrodite parent's back fur and trying to clamber around to get at the mammaries under "his" loose, formal overalls. "Hub scouting is important work, and it has been delayed long enough already. My scouts must be ready to resume service at a moment's notice." Kred wordlessly nudged the baby out of immediate sight, not acknowledging its presence in any way, though Nashira could hear it and the others peeping and see the occasional nose or paw-hand poke out despite Kred's best efforts to keep them behind his back. The Zeghryk's conviction that "Out of sight, out of mind" was an effective policy to cover up their out-of-control fecundity left Nashira convinced that the only things "out of mind" were the Zeghryk themselves.

"There are other scouts," said Rynyan.

"All of whom have more seniority—and more accrued vacation time—than Scout Wing." Nashira winced at the reminder. She'd been doing this job for eight years, but it had only been two months since the misfortune in the Ziovris system had led to Vekredi briefly declaring her dead, then hiring her back at a beginner's salary upon her legal resurrection. Even if she wanted to go to Earth, she could hardly afford any unpaid vacation time right now.

"Oh, come on, Kred," she wheedled. "I'm just wasting my

time here. I need to feel useful! And as long as you won't let me babysit your adorable little pups, there's nothing else for me to do." She craned her neck, trying to get a better look at them. "You know, I think they take after their mother. What is this, the third litter you spawned from her eggs? Or was she the sperm donor? Or do you mix and match?" *Watch it,* she warned herself. *Push him too far and he'll let you go just to get rid of you.*

But no; she'd insulted his sensibilities just enough. "Clearly your perceptions are compromised, Scout Wing. An undesirable quality in a Hub scout. I'll have to schedule you for another course of retraining sessions."

She feigned a sigh. "Oh, damn. I guess there's no getting out of it now. Sorry, Ryns, we did the best we could."

"Ahh, but what better training could there be than actual piloting?" Rynyan pressed irrepressibly. "And a return home could be just what she needs to clear her head. This will benefit both of us." He leaned forward, lowering his voice a tad. "And I'll be happy to provide whatever other benefits you may desire."

Kred's tiny eyes glared in contempt from behind his goggles. "You'll find, Mister Zynara, that not everyone is so easily swayed by money."

"Oh, money is merely a means to an end. And everyone has ends. For instance, I happen to own this lovely little life-bearing moon in the Draco Dwarf Galaxy... just plant life and a few small pollinators, a lovely place, but still pristine and unsettled. Why, we Sosyryn have far more territory than we'll ever need, and it's a pleasure to give it to those who can make good use of it."

"Don't be absurd," Kred huffed, pushing two more tiny heads back out of sight. "I don't know what scurrilous rumors you've heard, but our entirely stable and expansion-free population has no need for additional territory."

"Oh, of course not, of course not. I was thinking only of you, my good friend. You work so hard, managing this quaint little station, performing your vital service to the greater galaxy, yet you must put up with the constant distractions of maintenance crises and recalcitrant scouts and your—err—undersized neighbors constantly coming to visit," he said, waving toward the babies. "And there's nothing like wide open spaces to clear the mind and calm the nerves, am I right?"

Nashira's heart sank as Rynyan wheedled and bribed until Kred finally agreed to release her into his service. Not trusting herself to say anything, she left as promptly as she could. But Rynyan followed and said, "You know, that Vekredi fellow isn't nearly as bad as you make him out to be. Perhaps if you showed a little more respect for his sense of propriety about procreation—"

"Seriously? They breed like rabbits and pretend they're asexual. They're liars and hypocrites, and worse, they think the rest of us are morons! And they're a menace as long as they refuse to admit their population problem. If anyone deserves to have his sensibilities disrespected, it's Kred."

"Ah, well. At least you won't have to see him for a while. And you'll get to go home, see your family—"

She whirled on him. "You don't get it, do you? Do you think I'd put up with that *ngong gau*, risk my life and sanity doing Hub dives, if there were anything for me back on Earth? I'll take your friend as far as Earth orbit if it'll help her with her charity work, and if it gets me a vacation from Kred. But don't expect me to set foot on the dirt of that planet ever again."

2

"We are *so* glad you could come, Nashira," Andrea LaMacchia gushed for the fifth time since their arrival. "David has told us so much about you!" David's mother clutched Nashira's shoulders effusively. "But he never mentioned how beautiful you are!"

Nashira glared at David. "He didn't?!"

But David, as usual, was clueless, showing off the scenery out the window to Rynyan and Aytriaew. *Why did I let him talk me into this?* she wondered. At least there wasn't really any dirt. Far from the farm country she'd expected, the LaMacchias dwelt in a tall apartment building in Lafayette, Indiana. *Not much to farm here except wind,* she thought as she stared out at the thousands of spinning vanes that covered the drought-stricken landscape as far as the eye could see—though ending, of course, just outside the kilometer-high smart-mesh fence that surrounded the city, regulating its climate and dissipating the ferocious storms and tornadoes of the American Midwest, courtesy of Hub Network technology.

David's family was no *American Gothic* either. Andrea, a robust woman in her youthful mid-forties, was a biology professor at Purdue University and a single mother, sharing the apartment with David's half-brother Jason—a lanky 15-year-old currently lost in his own virtual world, eyes darting behind an alt-reality visor and hands forming arcane gestures in the air.

"Just be glad David's grandparents couldn't make it back from China in time," Andrea went on, "or you'd never hear the end of the matchmaking."

"Yeah... just as well," Nashira agreed, shaking off her disappointment. She was starting to come to terms with the fact that she was attracted to David for his innocence and kindness, but if he couldn't take his head out of the clouds long enough to notice the hot, experienced lady pilot standing right next to him, she wasn't going to embarrass herself trying to win him over.

"So David was raised mainly by his grandparents?" Rynyan asked.

"Oh, yes," Andrea replied as she handed Nashira a stack of salad bowls. Unconventional family or not, she was bent on fulfilling what she called her duty as an Italian mother, and she'd roped Nashira into helping set the table for the impending feast. "I was only sixteen when I had him, couldn't handle the responsibility," she went on, unabashed. "And his father was long gone—a member of one of those pulse bands I was a groupie for back then, I forget which."

"Which band?"

"Which member," she said, waggling her brows while David blushed. "Anyway, Mama and Papa took up the slack. David grew up thinking of me more as his big sister than his mother." Carrying a big pot of pasta to the table, refusing to let Nashira help, Andrea cried, "Come on, Jase, visor off! It's time to eat!"

"Aww, but mom, the Purity drones are closing in on Kansas City! This is important!"

"No war at the table! One of your little friends can handle it."

"His grandparents," Nashira echoed. "His doting, patient, indulgent grandparents raised him. That explains a lot."

Andrea returned with the pasta sauce and a plate of bread, which David took off her hands. "I've always believed as they did, that you should give your children the freedom to discover who they are instead of trying to make them who you want them to be. Jase, I'm not telling you again, visor off!"

Aytriaew stared as Jason grudgingly removed his visor. "War?" she asked. "Do you mean a game?"

"No, it's the real thing," Jason said. "Open-source war. Gamers make the best strategists, so they pay us to run the battles." He grimaced. "Except those Purity twaks, they don't play fair. They're shifting their drones toward a populated area! Real people could get hurt! That's not how you run a war!"

Nashira took her seat. She'd somewhat lost her taste for human food, but she had to admit, the sauce and bread smelled pretty good. "But don't you think if you'd pushed David to apply himself more, made him go out on his own earlier..."

"He'd have amounted to more?" Andrea laughed. "Oh, he may seem like a slow starter, but look where he is now! Living at the Hub, speaking for our planet. Working to make things better for everyone in the world. I couldn't be more proud." She handed Aytriaew her plate, saying, "Oh, speaking of which, dear, I took a look at your inventory list, and whoever briefed you on human medical needs deserves a whack upside the head—or however many heads they have. Some of what you've brought is useful, some could help a lot, but the quantities are low. The nanotech's programming is too generic for more than basic maintenance, and I'm afraid some of your biggest lots of medicines are downright toxic to humans."

"Oh," Aytriaew said, distracted. "That's... most disturbing to hear. I must have a talk with our suppliers before our next visit." She turned to Rynyan, her head spines tensing. "I thought the humits—ah, humans—had put an end to their wars in exchange for Network assistance. That's the usual way."

"Most of us, yes," Andrea said. "Nobody likes to advertise their family squabbles when company comes over."

"But not the prickin' Purity Party," Jason spat. "They're a religious militia. They all wear fox filters."

"What?" the Heurhot asked.

"Sensory censorship. Perceptual implants to block out anything that doesn't mesh with party ideology. Replaces it with fabricated input that reinforces their dogma. Far as they're concerned, aliens don't exist. You're all a leftist plot to discredit the Bible or something."

Aytriaew was horrified. "Are they widespread? Do they reach far?"

"Don't worry," Jason said. "They only control five states, and we're close to liberating Nebraska. Their strategy sucks.

Gaming's sinful, after all, so they don't go open-source."

"I meant the perceptual filters," the Heurhot said. "Are many humans so... unswayed by Network influence? Rejecting even the *idea* of alien life?"

"They're just a tiny fringe group," David assured her. "There are always some holdouts, but things are changing for the better."

Jason scoffed. "You would say that, half-bro. Me, I've fought them. Hell, I've traded flames with 'em. They're prickin' crazy. And more keep popping up. Lots o' people don't like aliens. Don't like havin' to depend on them. Makes 'em angry, willing to buy into the crazy."

Seeing Aytriaew's anxiety, Rynyan laughed and clapped her between her protruding scapulae. "Oh, but there are still so many more humans who truly appreciate all we do for them, believe me, dear. You'll see as our tour continues. Andrea, didn't you say David's grandparents are in China?"

"Yes, they're on a world tour of the great museums. Mom was a curator before she retired." Nashira blinked. Obviously David took after his father's side of the family.

"Well, then maybe we'll get to meet them after all," Rynyan told her. "I'm hoping we can make a stop in… that part of the world."

Nashira grabbed his feathery arm and spun him toward her. "You do *not* mean Hong Kong."

"Well, of course I'm dying to see the place where you were born. I've heard so much about the lovely canals."

"Believe me, you don't want to go there. It's a cesspool and they should've abandoned it to the floods."

"Oh, well, we'll see. Right now, I'm more interested in this intriguing recipe David's mother prepared."

Turning the conversation to food was enough to keep Andrea talking nonstop for quite some time. But Nashira wasn't so willing to be put off by Rynyan's diversionary tactics. After dinner, she managed to pull David aside, shutting the guest bedroom door behind them. "Listen, David—I just know Rynyan's plotting to track down my parents and spring some surprise reunion on me. You've gotta talk him out of it."

David frowned. "But why? Don't you miss your family?"

The door burst open behind them and Jason slipped in, shutting it again. "Sorry. Mom's gonna rope me into clearing the table and I've got a city to save." He slipped on the visor and inserted its earbuds. "Can't see or hear you, so you can talk or make out or whatever."

He resumed his spastic hand-waving, and Nashira hesitated. But David, evidently used to Jason's antics, was still looking to her for understanding. She sighed, pulling him to the other side of the room from Jason. "You don't—you can't know what it's like. Your mom, your grandparents, they value you for yourself. They want you around and don't even care that you're usel—I mean..." She winced, then took a deep breath. "There aren't a lot of options for Asian refugee families with teenage daughters. Being sold into effective slave labor as a maid overseas... that's usually the better alternative."

David was confused. "How could forced labor be better than..."

"*Fucking hell!*" Jason cried, making them whirl. "No, no, no, not there—ohh, pudz. Well, it's not like they needed that mall..."

Suddenly David's eyes widened in comprehension. "Ohh. *Oh!* Oh, whoa. Nashira, you don't mean..." He broke off at her steady gaze. "You do mean."

"I do mean. There are things a lot worse." Nashira sighed. "I guess that's how my parents saw it, like they were trying to do the best they could for me. But it wasn't good enough!" she went on angrily, pacing the room. "Nobody deserves that. They should've done more... shouldn't have settled for—"

"Aww, come on!" Jason cried. "Dude, shooting at a drone right when there's a school behind it? What's wrong with you, Felipe? We're the good guys! Lucky for you it wasn't three hours earlier!"

She broke off, gathered herself. "Anyway, I took matters into my own hands. Ran away... made it on my own for a few years. Eventually... managed to appropriate the means to get myself smuggled to the Hubpoint."

"'Appropriate?'"

"Let's just say I need to stay away from any security cameras in the vicinity of... ohh, call it Southeast Asia. In fact, probably best to avoid the whole Eastern Hemisphere."

David thought about it, then sighed. "Okay. I under—well, no, I don't understand. I think it's sad you don't want to see your folks, make amends. But... I respect your wishes, Nashira."

She looked down at the worn carpet. "Thanks."

"But why not just tell Rynyan yourself? If you explain it to him—"

"He could never understand!" she hissed through clenched teeth, coming in close to him. "He can't comprehend what poverty feels like, what desperation feels like. What helplessness feels like.

"More—I don't want to owe him a favor. And I can't let him see me... vulnerable."

David furrowed his brow. "You're letting *me* see you vulnerable."

She looked away. "Well... you're the only one I know would never take advantage."

"Aww..." His arms went around her, and Nashira stiffened in shock... then relaxed into it. Then hugged him back very tightly.

"Of course not," David said after a while. "That's what friends are for, right?"

She stiffened again, then pulled back, embarrassed with herself. She'd been this close to kissing him. "Friends. Right."

"Don't worry," he said. "I'll run interference with Rynyan." He clapped her shoulder and opened the door, leaving her with a final smile.

And Nashira found herself smiling a bit in spite of herself. "Hm. Friends..."

"Yeah!" cried Jason. "Let's see your fox filters spin *that*, you pricking twaks! Game *over!*" He pulled up his visor and glanced at Nashira. "Oh, pudz. I was hoping you'd at least have your top off by now."

Nashira smirked. "Don't know your brother that well, do you?"

3

David managed to divert Rynyan from tracking down Nashira's parents by shifting his mercurial attention onto a high-profile medical aid effort for injuries suffered by veterans of the ongoing Purity Crusade—mainly repetitive motion disorders and eyestrain from directing countless battle drones, but also some neurological conditions caused by enemy brain hacks, and the occasional burns or shrapnel injuries suffered by live humans who got too close to a battle site. Aside from the latter, the open-source war veterans lived all over the planet, drawn to the conflict more for the strategic challenge or the principle than for territorial allegiance, so Rynyan and Aytriaew were kept busy globe-hopping to ensure they didn't miss any photo opportunities while granting their benevolent, selfless aid.

But before long, Aytriaew insisted on returning to the Hub. The test run proved that Rynyan's methods for bypassing security checks were effective, so she was eager to get relief operations underway in earnest. Within a day of their return, her organization already had a large shipment of food printers and medical supplies ready for shipment to Gherv, the Zeghryk homeworld. Though Kred's people would never admit their population problem to outsiders (who were universally aware of it anyway), they weren't averse to accepting help with the resulting food shortages and health problems.

Things were just about back to normal for the Hub's denizens when the Soijt attacked again. This time, they infiltrated the Hubcomplex with a hundred and forty-seven elite, cybernetically enhanced shock troops who swiftly gained control of the central Shell (at least physically, though convincing its AIs to cooperate was another matter), with the goal of occupying and nationalizing the Hub in order to launch fleets of conquest throughout the greater galaxy. However, their generals back home had failed to grasp the true scale of the Hubcomplex: it was no mere outpost, but a whole hybrid civilization of millions of individuals from thousands of species, occupying dozens of immense ring habitats that circled the Hub, plus numerous statite fortresses, defense fleets, and weapons batteries run by the civilizations that cooperated in enforcing Hub security. Expecting to gain the ultimate high ground, the Soijt troopers had instead found themselves both literally and figuratively surrounded by the entire galaxy.

To salve their warrior pride, the Soijt had threatened to blow up the Shell and themselves with it, so that if they couldn't have it, no one else could. But they found themselves barraged by testimonials from thousands of cultures telling them of the immense benefits their world could gain by participating peacefully in Network trade—plus reminders that a new Shell could always be built around the Hub itself, that indestructible knot in reality that seemed to be a natural property of the greater galaxy's center of mass. Even some of these hardened, proud cyborg warriors resisted their no-surrender programming long enough to relay the messages back home and request further orders, and before long, the Soijt government agreed to open negotiations for the "repatriation" of the Shell (whose governing consciousnesses mutually agreed to stand down from their ongoing efforts to suffocate, crush, immolate, jettison, and otherwise eliminate the invaders—though they were already holding most of the dead in stasis for eventual revival once the crisis was resolved).

Still, the occupation of the Shell meant more downtime for Nashira, and she found herself oddly pleased when David agreed to help with some delayed maintenance on her Hubdiver. Helping her lug the ship's heavy cryotank to the quantelope care facility wasn't as big a favor as diverting Rynyan from finding her parents, but in the wake of that, it felt good to have someone she knew she could rely on, even for the little things. Although refreshing the quantelopes' connection to their entanglemates was no trivial matter, since the alternative might be getting stranded in deep intergalactic space with no way to call the Hub for retrieval.

Once they hooked up the airlock, David watched with fascination as the tank's purple-furred occupants skittered their way into the larger terrarium. He used his sleeve to wipe away the condensation so he could see better as Nashira's 'lopes approached their entanglemates and began rubbing horns. "Ooh! Is that it? Is that how they renew the entanglement?"

Nashira chuckled. "Not exactly. Keep watching."

David took her advice for a few moments… but then his eyes widened and he blushed. "Umm… maybe we should give them some privacy?"

She laughed louder. "Why so surprised? You know how they work. Liquid ammonia metabolism, Bose-Einstein condensates in their blood. You want 'em entangled, there's gotta be some exchange of fluids." Nashira wiggled her eyebrows. "And these guys are kind of overdue. I like to put it off so Kred has to pester me about it."

David frowned. "But you hate it when he pesters you."

"But I just can't resist the look on his face when he tries to order me to mate the 'lopes without talking about sex. You can hear his little mole teeth grinding halfway across the Hubstation!"

"Ahh, how I love to hear you discussing sex!" Rynyan breezed into the room, sliding an arm around her shoulders. "Is all this mating giving you any ideas, my dear?"

"Why, yes," she said, smiling up at him sweetly. "I'm having a very enjoyable thought about releasing that purge valve next to your nether regions and spraying them with liquid ammonia. I know how much you crave new sensations."

"Ah," Rynyan said, judiciously retreating to the other side of the tank. "Well, I'm afraid I didn't actually come to seduce you today. I hate to disappoint you, my dear, but I'm afraid I'm simply too exhausted at the moment. Aytriaew is rather insatiable."

"I thought you weren't interested in her anymore," David said.

"Well, I'm not, but it's not about what *I* want, you know. Full access to my body is part of the terms of our contract. After all, it wouldn't be much of an act of charity if I didn't grant her the ultimate boon, would it?" He preened his mane.

Nashira stared in disgust. "Doesn't that make you feel... used?"

"Oh, absolutely! Nothing so bracing as self-sacrifice. It's rekindled my excitement about her. Oh, but don't worry, Nashira," he went on, reaching out to pat the hand she was too stunned to pull away in time. "Once my dealings with Aytriaew are over, I'll be yours for the using once again. That will give you time to think up some very tawdry and creative ways to use me, I'm sure."

It was all Nashira could do not to lose her breakfast. Luckily the 'lopes had finished their business, so she didn't have to face yet another reminder of sex. She used the waldos to coax her 'lopes back into the tank, and she and David began the long slog back to the ship. Rynyan "helped," so he claimed, by using his superior height to keep an eye out for obstacles. "Anyway, Nashira, the reason I did come to see you is that Aytriaew is making more relief runs to Gherv, and I convinced her to hire you as a pilot!" He preened. "I'm sure you can think of ways to thank me later, once we're both in more receptive moods."

"Wow, Nashira, that's great!" David said. "You get to fly again, and you can do some real good too. Hey, we could even visit my family again next time she makes a delivery to Earth."

She resisted the urge to scoff, not wanting to shatter the idealism she was increasingly learning to appreciate. She knew a con artist when she saw one, and Aytriaew wasn't even a particularly subtle one. The Heurhot had obviously never heard of Earth or humans before that day in the restaurant, but had feigned interest in Rynyan's pet planet to win his support, then used the trip to Earth as a trial run for Rynyan's methods of getting her contraband, whatever it was, past Hub customs.

"As a matter of fact," Rynyan said, "Aytriaew has told me that since she learned of that terrible war from your brother, she's become even more concerned for your people's plight and intends to make sure you get the attention you deserve, once she's completed her efforts with the Zeghryk."

"Hey, that's great!" David said.

I'll believe it when I see it, Nashira thought. Still, the money had been good the last time. And it didn't bother her that Aytriaew was playing Rynyan. If others could benefit from his petty, self-serving charity, that was fine, and if he ended up humiliated when the truth came out, maybe that would do him—or at least those around him—some good. And who knew? Maybe if she found out what the Heurhot's real racket was, there'd be a way she could profit further from it. "Okay," she said. "Tell Aytriaew she's got herself a pilot."

> Conditions in the Zeghryk's home system were just as Nashira had imagined—every habitable body flooded with Zeghryk, most of them children, though even here the authorities insisted they were just adults of small stature. The overcrowded colonies reminded Nashira of some of the refugee camps where she'd grown up after her family had been driven out of Hong Kong—back in that final frenzy of wars as nations and religions jockeyed for positions of power in the global order that would stand once the peace treaties required for full Network membership were signed. It was almost enough to prompt sympathy for Kred's people, and the hope that maybe Aytriaew's relief flights here were as legitimate as they seemed—until she reminded herself that the Zeghryk's miseries were self-inflicted, their own fault for refusing any sane amount of population control. Not that humans were much better in that regard, she admitted. But then, she didn't have much sympathy for humans either.
>
> Still, it was a relief when Aytriaew told her that her second trip to Gherv would be the last. A relief, but a surprise. "From what I saw, they still need a lot of help."
>
> "Oh, don't worry," Aytriaew told her. "I can

guarantee that the resources we've provided will have a lasting effect on their population crisis."

Nashira found the Heurhot's words puzzling, but soon forgot about them as she resumed her Hub scout duties for Kred. Weeks of tedious life-risking passed, every dive to random new coordinates carrying as much chance of materializing inside a planet or a star as of discovering something new and lucrative; but the probabilities remained overwhelmingly in favor of discovering another new stretch of intergalactic nothingness each and every time. Only David and Rynyan's frequent accompaniment as the young human continued his futile and unqualified studies of Hub physics brought any variety to the experience. Between dives, she sparred with Kred to extract each credit she was owed from his greedy little paws, traded banter and boasts with her fellow Hub scouts while resenting those few who actually stumbled upon anything interesting, and passed her time with the occasional casual lovers who, unlike David, actually noticed she was a woman—or at least weren't too wholesome and easily distracted to do anything about it.

And then she heard the news from her fellow scouts when she returned from a particularly long and tedious dive session, one she'd taken alone, since David and Rynyan had been busy making plans with Aytriaew for the Earth relief missions—missions that Nashira still wasn't convinced would actually happen. According to the buzz around the Hubstation, something had happened in the Gherv system. Some crisis had the Zeghryk in a frenzy, yet they wouldn't tell anyone else what was wrong—meaning it had to involve reproduction somehow. Non-Zeghryk visitors, upon being asked to leave the system, brought rumors of an epidemic of infertility—the worst fate the Zeghryk could imagine, even though they insisted it was their normal state of affairs.

Soon, an anonymous press release rocked the Network:

"We are a group of concerned denizens of Network civilization, representing many worlds. For too long, we have watched the Network tolerate the threat the Zeghryk population explosion posed to the Zeghryk themselves and to biospheres and populations throughout the greater galaxy. We have watched them indulge the Zeghryk's criminal refusal to admit the crisis and take responsibility for its resolution. And so we have chosen to take that responsibility on their behalf.

"The entire population of the Gherv system, and that of many other worlds inhabited by Zeghryk, has been infected with an adaptive nanovirus which has rendered all Zeghryk permanently sterile. No Zeghryk exposed to this nanovirus will be capable of conceiving young. Those pregnancies in progress will be allowed to come to term, but no new Zeghryk embryos will be conceived. The nanovirus is hyper-mutating; cure one strain and another will take its place.

"We have no wish to see the Zeghryk species exterminated—merely limited. Those who now live can have their lives prolonged by Network medicine; indeed, they already have, which is part of the problem. Perhaps, in time, every strain of the virus will be cured; but by then, we believe, the Zeghryk population will have been reduced to a reasonable size—and hopefully will have overcome its addiction to unfettered procreation. We have acted for the good of all species in the Hub Network, including the Zeghryk themselves. We hope one day they—or their manageable number of descendants—will forgive us for what we have done.

"But if they don't... well, we're comfortable with that too."

The Network's first reaction was disbelief. The Gherv system was on the fringes of the Large Magellanic Cloud, remote from any other inhabited world, so the only way such a virus could have been delivered was through the Hub. And Hub security would never have let a bioweapon go through. The Hub had protected every world in the Network from invasion and violation for thousands of years; it simply couldn't happen.

But Hub journalists were as nosy as the Earthly breed, and soon enough the proof came: the nanovirus was real, and its effects on the Zeghryk were exactly as advertised. Someone had effectively conquered the entire species without firing a shot.

And Nashira's heart sank as she realized she'd helped Aytriaew do it.

At first she tried to convince herself that the Zeghryk had it coming. If they couldn't be bothered to manage their population, then it was a good thing somebody had.

But then she arrived at Kred's office and found him packed up and on his way out, babies still clinging to his back and clambering over the large bags he held under his arms. "You're leaving?"

"Your powers of observation are finally approaching adequacy, Scout Wing," Vekredi replied with annoyance as she blocked the door. "At least, I will be leaving, once you cease being an impediment."

"Where... where are you going?"

"Not that it's any concern of yours, but I'm returning home."

She gaped. "To Gherv?"

"Again you approach comprehension of the self-evident."

"But... but you can't! Kred, if you go back there, you'll be infected! You'll never be able to have kids again!"

His beady eyes flashed. "Scout Wing, really! I will not miss your constant vulgarity."

To her own surprise, she knelt to be closer to his eye level. "Look, Kred, I know you don't like to talk about it, but... do you really want to do this? Have you really thought it through?"

"There is nothing to think through, Scout Wing. My... people need me, so I go. It is as simple as that."

She squeezed her eyes shut. *Of course it is.* They couldn't confide in anyone else, so whom could they turn to except family? And how could anyone who loved family as much as Mokak Vekredi possibly do less than make the ultimate sacrifice for them? She suddenly saw her employer in an entirely new light. "Kred... listen... you know, people would be willing to help if you'd just talk to them. So if, if there's anything you need to talk about..."

Those unblinking eyes pierced her as they never had in eight years of trying. "Tell me, Scout Wing. What could possibly make you imagine that if I were to seek sympathy from anyone, it would be *you?!*"

He pushed his way past her and out the door. Once he was gone, Nashira took a shuddering breath. "No, you're right. And you don't know the fucking half of it."

4

David LaMacchia did not find Rynyan's private tesseract suite in Hubstation 3742 the most suitable place to work on planning relief missions with Aytriaew and their mutual Sosyryn sponsor. The suite of four-dimensionally interconnected rooms was lavishly appointed and filled with distractions, and David doubted there was a single surface in the suite on which Rynyan hadn't had sex with someone. Still, Rynyan had insisted on "donating" the space (well, hyperspace) for their use, for Aytriaew would not tolerate working in the run-down Hubstation's sparsely appointed meeting rooms. For someone so fond of charity, David thought, Aytriaew was surprisingly uncomfortable with roughing it.

Still, Aytriaew's passionate commitment to the work itself was undeniable and infectious. Even Nashira had gotten drawn into the charitable spirit, no matter how much she pretended her motives were purely mercenary. Of course, he couldn't blame his Hub scout friend for her refusal to set foot in Rynyan's suite; David knew Rynyan would never attempt to impose on her against her will, but still, it was probably best not to do anything the Sosyryn would take as encouragement. But it pleased David that Nashira was with him on this, at least in spirit.

So David was more than a little surprised when Nashira interrupted his latest planning session with Rynyan and Aytriaew by storming into the suite, screaming *"You!"*, punching the Heurhot in the face, then tackling her to the ground and continuing the assault. He cried Nashira's name in dismay as the two females rolled into the next room.

"What... what is the meaning of this?" Aytriaew gasped,

trying to fend off the smaller human's blows.

"Oh, I know this!" Rynyan cried, clapping his hands as he and David followed them through the door. "It's an Earth custom called a catfight. I've studied it extensively in their pr0n," he went on, somehow managing to pronounce the zero. "You're supposed to rip each other's clothes off violently while screaming insults, then start having sex while David and I watch." Aytriaew had managed to pull herself free and make a run for the ramp down to the next level, but Nashira shrieked and pounced on her, causing them both to tumble down the incline. "Oh, Nashira, I'm honored by the tribute!" Rynyan called after them.

But David was already following them down. By the time he reached the base of the ramp, Nashira was chasing Aytriaew from room to room at high speed. David tried to run after them, but he hadn't made it through two doors before Aytriaew shoved past him *from behind*. It slowed her enough for Nashira to catch up and tackle her to the floor of the kitchen compartment—evoking a whoop of glee from Rynyan, who was coming *up* a spiral staircase from the level below.

David shook off his confusion at the mysteries of hyperspace geometry and waded in to pull the pilot off the Heurhot. "Nashira, calm down! Tell us what's going on. What's she done?"

"What's she *done?!*" Nashira snarled, whirling to face him. "Can't you idiots put the pieces together? This bitch got Rynyan to smuggle her 'relief shipments' past Hub security to the Gherv system!" At their continued silence, she went on, "Don't you see? She's the one behind the nanovirus! She sterilized an entire race!" She blinked, unwonted moisture in her sleek, dark eyes. "And we helped her do it!"

David was speechless, but Rynyan filled the void. "Nashira, don't be ridiculous. I did have her shipments checked. I know what was in them."

"But you wouldn't know what to look for, not like Hub customs would. Think about it. She made, what, half a dozen trips before the sterilization kicked in? I heard of terrorists on Earth doing this during the Final Wars. You use modular nanotech, sneak it past security one piece at a time, so they look innocuous till they self-assemble."

Aytriaew had regained her feet and was brushing back her head-spines. "This is an outrageous allegation, Nashira. You know me."

"I've known from the start you were using Rynyan to smuggle something. I thought—" Her voice broke. "I thought it'd be harmless. But now... damn it, you told me yourself we'd had a 'lasting effect on their population crisis.' You confessed it, you—" Nashira called her something in Cantonese that rhymed with "how high." David had a feeling he didn't want to know what it meant.

But he was remembering how shocked the Heurhot had been about the Purity War, and particularly about the humans who were in denial about aliens. So he turned to her and solemnly asked, "Aytriaew... what were you planning to have us ship to Earth?"

The Heurhot turned to Rynyan, stroking his feathery mane. "Rynyan, dear, please get your little humits to behave! Surely you can see how ludicrous all this is."

"Why... yes, of course. It must be. I'd never let myself be a party to anything like this—the consequences to my tally would be disastrous if I were involved in anything that *hurt* people!" Rynyan grasped her shoulders and met her gaze intently. "It *is* untrue, isn't it? If I check that shipment to Earth with extra care, I won't find anything amiss, will I?"

She gave a Heurhot-style laugh that even David could tell was nervous. "Well, there are certain ... supplements to the medicines that could ... conceivably ... be incorporated into some kind of harmful nanovirus *if* certain other components were delivered separately. Well, at least I suppose they could be, not that I know anything about such matters...."

David shook his head in dismay. "I can't believe this. It's true, isn't it? You used my friends to hurt people... and now you're gonna do something to Earth!"

"No," Rynyan insisted. "No, this can't be true. It would ruin me!"

"Is that still all you can think about?!" Nashira cried in

disgust. "What about your friends? Look at David. Look at him! From the start, he's trusted you, relied on you, and look what you did!" She grasped David's shoulders from behind and pushed him forward in demonstration. "Look at his face! It's a sad face! He's an innocent little puppy dog and you made him sad! How could you do that?" she hectored, shaking David vigorously to underscore her point.

"No," Rynyan said. "I only tried to help. That's what I do! Aytriaew, tell me I helped!"

"You did," the elegant Heurhot assured him. "The galaxy will be much better off in the long term now that the Zeghryk scourge is ended. And the Zeghryk will survive... some of them... probably... and they'll be better off too! Eventually."

Rynyan was wavering. "But what's wrong with humanity?" he asked. "Well, aside from the obvious, but we've put up with worse before."

"Hey?!" David said.

"Wasn't it clear? Not only are they overpopulated too, not only do they still wage war—but they even deny that we exist! How can we guide them, manage them, if they won't even acknowledge us? First they reshape their own senses to change reality, then they try to change their own world by force—what might they do to the galaxy in order to eliminate what they don't believe in?"

"Not like you'd know anything about that," Nashira spat.

David stepped forward, meeting his Sosyryn benefactor's eyes pleadingly. "Rynyan, you have to turn her in. I know it would get you in trouble, but it's the right thing to do, and I know you have that in you. I believe you care enough about Earth, about your friends, to do what's right when it really matters."

Rynyan preened his mane nervously as he thought. "Yes," he said, then less tentatively, "Yes, it could work. Exposing a dangerous conspiracy, saving the people of Earth and other worlds from further depredations—that would be such a triumph of benevolence that it would more than make up for any harm I inadvertently caused! Why, yes, if I spin this right I could—"

David smacked him hard in the face. Nashira gasped—or was it a laugh? "Listen to yourself! Nashira was right about you all along. You don't care about me, about Earth! All your charity, it's just to make you feel good. You don't think about anyone but yourself, and that's why you let this, this monster get away with what she did! And you almost made Earth pay the same price! I can't believe I ever trusted you."

"But... David, no, that's not what I meant. I'm just trying to see the best in things, like I always do. I always try to make things better."

David studied him for a moment. "I know you do," he conceded, anger giving way to sadness. "But you need to start thinking about what the right reasons are for doing that. You need to think about the consequences to other people, not just your tally."

He turned and started to leave, but Rynyan trailed him. "What about the consequences to you if you walk away? You need me, so I take care of you! I won't stop doing that even though we had this fight. Please, let me prove I mean well."

David turned back. "I will. You can prove it by turning Aytriaew in."

Aytriaew stepped forward, drawing a firearm from her pocket. "I'm afraid I can't let you do—"

"Oh, shut up," Nashira said, following it with a roundhouse punch that sent both gun and wielder flying to land uselessly on the floor.

"I, ah, I can do that," Rynyan said. "I *will* do that. And then—"

"And then we'll see," David replied. "But I'm through taking charity from you, Rynyan. The cost is too high."

David turned and left Rynyan there, not looking back. Although he did have to look around a bit to find his way to the suite's exit.

But soon he saw Nashira strolling alongside him down the hotel corridor, clutching her bruised hand. He took it in his and began to stroke it soothingly. "Let's get you something for the pain."

"Ohh, it's a good pain," she assured him. "I like this pain.

But—you don't have to let go."

"Okay." They walked hand in hand for a while.

"So what are you gonna do now, without Rynyan to pay your room and board?"

David sighed. "I guess... I'll just have to get..." He swallowed. "A job."

Nashira reached up, pulled his head down, and kissed him on the cheek. "What was that for?" he asked afterward.

She grinned, and it was the warmest, prettiest expression he'd ever seen on her face. "Keep going the way you're going, kid," she said. "You'll figure it out eventually."

"Okay," David said, looking forward to that day. After a while, he asked, "Umm, so do you think maybe I could try out for a Hub scout job like yours?"

"Oh, no way in hell! Your mum told me about your driving test."

"Good point. Oh, that reminds me, I've been meaning to ask: Hub scouting's a risky job, so why not use robot probes? Why do they need living scouts at all?"

"To keep the quantelopes company."

"Ahh. That explains it."

HUB NETWORK NEWS BRIEFING

ND 23,409/7821-04.HELIOTROPE (EXCERPT)

Rynyan Zynara ad Surynyyyyyy'a has done it again! For the second time this quarter, the handsome Sosyryn philanthropist/adventurer has exposed a major scandal. Hot on the heels of exposing the Ziovris government's concealment of a second Hubpoint in their system—only the fourth time in Network history that two Hubpoints have been found in such proximity—Rynyan has now blown open the conspiracy of "concerned denizens" behind the shocking sterilization attack on the Zeghryk civilization of Hubstation 3742. The leader of the conspiracy, a Heurhot female named Hwaieur-7 Aytriaew, is now in custody, and investigators are in the process of tracking down her co-conspirators.

According to Rynyan's testimony, Ms. Hwaieur took advantage of the Sosyryn's famous generosity to smuggle in a modular nanovirus under the guise of a charity operation funded by Rynyan. With his characteristic modesty, Rynyan has insisted that the credit for the exposure of the conspiracy should go to a Hub scout named Bringer-of-Good-News Airfoil, a junior-species female occasionally employed as a pilot by both Rynyan and Ms. Hwaieur. Reportedly Ms. Airfoil's planet, Urt, was one of several worlds targeted for biological attack by Hwaieur's organization, also including the Soijt homeworld and the Deathsphere of Idge. Ms. Airfoil is a known sexual associate of Rynyan's, one of the many females spoken of in his explicit public journal, though Rynyan has recently deleted the more salacious entries. We can surmise that his attempt to share credit with her is yet another of his many and varied acts of charity.

We contacted Ms. Airfoil for her reactions to the heroic feat Rynyan undertook in her name and her opinions on his famed sexual prowess, but her response proved unsuitable for broadcast. Perhaps she's simply overwhelmed with gratitude that the Hub Network came through for her beloved Urt once again.

AFTERWORD: MAKE YOURSELF AT HUB

Once, I formulated a theory about science fiction sitcoms. This was before *Futurama*, before I saw *Red Dwarf*. All the space-based sitcoms I'd seen up to then, from the best (Buck Henry's *Quark*) to the worst (UPN's *Homeboys in Outer Space*), seemed to fail, and my belief was that it was because they were all farces and spoofs, set in worlds that merely mocked SF tropes rather than having any integrity of their own. A spoof could be entertaining as a movie or a novel, but it seemed to me that for an ongoing series to win an audience, its world and characters had to be believable enough for viewers to invest in. When I did see *Red Dwarf* and *Futurama*, they supported this belief; while both shows had a lot of spoof in them, they managed to build interesting universes of their own, to go beyond simply making fun of science fiction to telling stories that actually *were* science fiction, that worked as speculative tales in their own right while being told in a funny way.

So I decided I'd like to see an SF sitcom whose premise was as credible and well-developed as any dramatic SF universe, but whose focus was on humorous characters and situations within that universe. After all, there's nothing intrinsically absurd about a sheriff in a small town, an Army hospital in the Korean War, a taxi company in New York, or a radio psychologist in Seattle. Most sitcoms depict naturalistic situations and derive their humor from characters and events. Why couldn't an SF sitcom do the same? There's plenty of humor potential in a plausibly created SF universe. Just imagine the cultural clashes and misunderstandings between species, or the ways that technology could go wrong.

But an SF sitcom would naturally be under budgetary constraints. Perhaps the best approach would be to emulate sitcoms like *Taxi* and *Wings* by using a transportation nexus as the setting—a place that many different people pass through, allowing a wide range of stories while staying on a few standing sets. What if it's *the* transportation nexus, the only means of FTL travel known to exist? How would it operate? What would be the ramifications? Once I had the idea of the Hub, it spawned many rich possibilities.

The sets for a sitcom couldn't be too elaborate, so why not make it the most run-down, least technologically advanced section of this great interstellar nexus? After all, if Earth were new to the interstellar community, it might not rate classier facilities. And humor often comes from failure and frustration.

But you need hope, too. If humanity's so lowly in interstellar society, maybe the hero wants to prove humanity's worth. A nice, optimistic, humanist message. But it needs a comedic twist, so maybe the hero's a lovable loser, a guy with lots of hope but questionable qualifications. And what better foil for him than a cynical leading lady who's been around the block a few times? Along with a helpful alien who represents the brighter, more idealized side of galactic life—and its comical downside.

But not long after I came up with the Hub universe, I decided I didn't have any interest in moving to Hollywood and pursuing a TV career. Thus, it became a prose series instead, eventually appearing in *Analog Science Fiction and Fact*—"The Hub of the Matter" in the March 2010 issue, "Home is Where the Hub Is" in the December 2010 issue, and "Make Hub, Not War" not appearing until the November 2013 issue.

My long-term plan from the start was to do enough stories to collect into a fix-up novel. But when I wrote "Make Hub, Not War," I decided to take things in a direction that brought some closure to certain story threads, making the first three novelettes work as a trilogy of sorts. And the rise of e-book publishing has created a new market for novella-length publications. So rather than waiting however many years it took to sell a novel's worth of stories, I decided to go ahead and release this compilation now. This has given me the opportunity to correct the errors in the original *Analog* editions ("The Hub of the Matter" somehow got published without my final corrections, and I got the Zeghryk species' name wrong in "Home is Where the Hub Is"), to tweak a few words here and there, and to add new material, both within and between the stories, to flesh out the environment and characters a bit more. Essentially, nothing has been removed except a few redundant expository passages in the latter two stories, lines that were written to be expendable for just such an occasion.

A few acknowledgments: Thanks to *Analog* editor Stanley Schmidt and his successor Trevor Quachri for buying the original stories, to Trevor and Emily Hockaday for their editorial assistance, to David Niall Wilson for agreeing to publish this collection, and to Aaron Rosenberg for putting me in touch with David.

The Hub, a single point that can connect instantaneously to anywhere in the galaxy, was indirectly inspired by the title object from "The Aleph," a 1949 story by Jorge Luis Borges—a single point containing all other points, allowing an observer to see anything in the universe. I say "indirectly" because I first learned of the concept from the *Star Trek* novel *The Starship Trap* by Mel Gilden. Meanwhile, the Hub's tesseract suites owe a lot to Robert A. Heinlein's story "…And He Built a Crooked House," while Wing's—err, Rynyan's Rings are influenced by the Smoke Ring from Larry Niven's novels *The Integral Trees* and *The Smoke Ring*.

The Milky Way galaxy's dark matter halo is believed to make up 95 percent of the mass of the galaxy, which is why it made sense to me to place the Hub at its center of mass rather than that of the visible galaxy. It's estimated to extend roughly 100,000 parsecs in radius. The lists I consulted when I wrote "The Hub of the Matter" must have been incomplete or outdated, since there are more than eight satellite galaxies currently known to exist within that radius. We can reconcile this by assuming that no inhabited worlds have yet been discovered in any of them, so that none of them are counted as part of the Hub Network. Most of the Milky Way's satellites are dwarf elliptical or irregular galaxies, which have little active star formation and are unlikely to have many habitable planetary systems as a result. Most species in the Hub Network must come from the Milky Way or the Magellanic Clouds, but there are probably settlements in all the galaxies in the network.

Further story discussion and notes can be found on my website at:

   http://home.fuse.net/ChristopherLBennett/Originalfiction.html#Hub.

ABOUT THE AUTHOR

Christopher L. Bennett is a lifelong resident of Cincinnati, Ohio, with a B.S. in Physics and a B.A. in History from the University of Cincinnati. A fan of science and science fiction since age five, he has sold original short fiction to magazines such as *Analog Science Fiction and Fact* and *Buzzy Mag* and is one of Pocket Books' most prolific and popular authors of Star Trek tie-in fiction, including the epic Next Generation prequel *The Buried Age*, the ongoing Star Trek: Enterprise—*Rise of the Federation* series, and the Star Trek: *Department of Temporal Investigations* series. His original novel *Only Superhuman*, perhaps the first hard science fiction superhero novel, was voted Library Journal's SF/Fantasy Debut of the Month for October 2012. His homepage and Written Worlds blog can be found at http://christopherlbennett.wordpress.com/, and his Facebook author page is at https://www.facebook.com/ChristopherLBennettAuthor

Curious about other Crossroad Press books?
Stop by our site:
http://store.crossroadpress.com
We offer quality writing
in digital, audio, and print formats.

Enter the code FIRSTBOOK
to get 20% off your first order from our store!
Stop by today!

Made in the USA
Monee, IL
15 July 2020